"In tod[...] where every ending is a happy one."
—*New York Times* and *USA TODAY*
Bestselling Author Elizabeth Bevarly

Look for all six
Special 30th Anniversary Collectors' Editions
from some of our most popular authors.

**TEMPTED BY HER INNOCENT KISS**
by Maya Banks
with "Never Too Late" by Brenda Jackson

**BEHIND BOARDROOM DOORS**
by Jennifer Lewis
with "The Royal Cousin's Revenge"
by Catherine Mann

**THE PATERNITY PROPOSITION**
by Merline Lovelace
with "The Sheik's Virgin" by Susan Mallery

**A TOUCH OF PERSUASION**
by Janice Maynard
with "A Lover's Touch" by Brenda Jackson

**A FORBIDDEN AFFAIR**
by Yvonne Lindsay
with "For Love or Money" by Elizabeth Bevarly

**CAUGHT IN THE SPOTLIGHT**
by Jules Bennett
with "Billionaire's Baby" by Leanne Banks

\* \* \*

Find Harlequin Desire on Facebook,
www.facebook.com/HarlequinDesire,
or on Twitter, @desireeditors!

Dear Reader,

I can scarcely believe it's Desire's 30th anniversary! I still remember so clearly coming home from college classes to discover that the mailman left me a box full of those little red books. Invariably I'd immediately put aside my assigned reading to dive into one of those instead. After days filled with 500 and 600 level literature courses full of "classics" where the heroines never seemed to have much of a happy ending, it was so refreshing to read stories about powerful women in charge of their own lives and destinies being rewarded for their strength and integrity by finding true love.

I always knew I wanted to be a writer. It's why I majored in English. But from the day I read my first Desire title (Dixie Browning's *The Hawk and the Honey*), I knew what *kind* of book I wanted to write. I wanted to write for Desire. It was such a rush to see my first one in print nearly twenty years ago. It's a rush to see one in print today, I confess. I love knowing I'm part of such a rich literary history. I love hearing, as a writer, from women who adore the books as readers as much as I did—and still do. It just makes me feel as if I'm part of this amazing circle of life and a member of a community filled with, well, powerful women in charge of their own lives and destinies.

Thank you, Desire, for thirty wonderful years of reading romance and twenty fabulous years of writing it. I can't wait to see what the next thirty have in store!

Happy reading!

Elizabeth

# YVONNE LINDSAY

## A FORBIDDEN AFFAIR

ISBN-13: 978-0-373-73160-2

A FORBIDDEN AFFAIR

Recycling programs
for this product may
not exist in your area.

# CONTENTS

**Books by Yvonne Lindsay**

Harlequin Desire

*Bought: His Temporary Fiancée* #2078
*The Pregnancy Contract* #2117
††*The Wayward Son* #2141
††*A Forbidden Affair* #2147

Silhouette Desire

\**The Boss's Christmas Seduction* #1758
\**The CEO's Contract Bride* #1776
\**The Tycoon's Hidden Heir* #1788
*Rossellini's Revenge Affair* #1811
*Tycoon's Valentine Vendetta* #1854
*Jealousy & A Jewelled Proposition* #1873
*Claiming His Runaway Bride* #1890
†*Convenient Marriage, Inconvenient Husband* #1923
†*Secret Baby, Public Affair* #1930
†*Pretend Mistress, Bona Fide Boss* #1937
*Defiant Mistress, Ruthless Millionaire* #1986
\*\**Honor-Bound Groom* #2029
\*\**Stand-In Bride's Seduction* #2038
\*\**For the Sake of the Secret Child* #2044

\*New Zealand Knights
†Rogue Diamonds
\*\*Wed at Any Price
††The Master Vintners

Other titles by this author available in ebook format.

## YVONNE LINDSAY

New Zealand born, to Dutch immigrant parents, Yvonne Lindsay became an avid romance reader at the age of thirteen. Now, married to her "blind date" and with two fabulous children, she remains a firm believer in the power of romance. Yvonne feels privileged to be able to bring to her readers the stories of her heart. In her spare time, when not writing, she can be found with her nose firmly in a book, reliving the power of love in all walks of life. She can be contacted via her website, www.yvonnelindsay.com.

Dear Reader,

Have you ever worked your butt off for something, or someone, only to feel that your hard work was never recognized or appreciated? It's a fact of life for many of us as we strive to always do our best. Whether we do it for ourselves or for another, recognition is often validation that we're doing something worthwhile.

For Nicole Wilson, in *A Forbidden Affair,* it's as if her life's work has been for nothing when her long-estranged brother returns to her father's side and usurps her position not only at home, but in the business she's wanted to be a part of all her life. Suddenly everything Nicole had always assumed was hers wasn't. What happens next is a roller-coaster ride of emotion and passion until Nicole finally gets what she most deserves.

I hope you enjoy this sequel to *The Wayward Son* and that you'll keep an eye out for further stories in The Master Vintners yet to come.

Happy reading!

Yvonne Lindsay

To the memory of Sandra Hyde (writing as Sandra Hyatt) and the legacy of her friendship.

# A FORBIDDEN AFFAIR

Yvonne Lindsay

# One

Nicole's hands shook uncontrollably as she tried to fit her key into the ignition. Damn, she dropped it again. She swiped the key ring up off the floor of her classic Benz, and gave up driving as a bad joke. If she couldn't even get the key in the ignition, how on earth did she expect to drive?

She got out of the car, slammed the door hard and swiped her cell phone from her bag. Thank goodness she'd had the presence of mind to grab the designer leather pouch from the hall table after her grand exit from the family dinner to end all family dinners.

Her high heels clipped a staccato beat as she marched down the well-lit driveway of her family home to the street, calling a taxi service as she went. Fine tremors shook her body as she waited for the car to arrive. The chill air of the autumn night made her glad she hadn't had a chance to change out of her tailored wool suit when she'd arrived home from work earlier.

Her father had requested that she dress up for dinner in honor of a special announcement he'd planned to make, but by the time she'd gotten home, there just hadn't been enough time. She hadn't thought her father would mind that she'd chosen to put in the extra time at the office instead of rushing home to get ready. After all, if anyone should understand her drive to devote her time and energy to Wilson Wines then surely it would be Charles Wilson, founder and CEO. Her father had invested most of his life into the business he had built, and she'd always intended to follow in his footsteps.

Until tonight.

Another rush of anger infused her. How dare her father belittle her like that, and in front of a virtual stranger, as well? Who cared if that stranger was her long-lost brother, Judd. Two and a half decades after their parents' bitter divorce had split their family in half, what right did he have to come back and lay claim to the responsibilities that were supposed to be *hers?* She clenched her jaw tight and bit back the scream of frustration that threatened to claw its way out of her throat. She couldn't lose it now. Not when she had just discovered that she was the only person she had left to rely on.

Even her best friend, colleague and life-long confidante, Anna, had shown her true colors when she'd arrived home in New Zealand from Adelaide, Australia, late last week with Judd in tow. Sure, she'd tried to convince Nicole that she'd only been following Charles's orders to find Judd and bring about a reconciliation, but Nicole knew where Anna's loyalties lay, and they certainly weren't with her. If they were,

Anna wouldn't have kept the truth from her about what Charles planned to use as Judd's incentive.

A painful twist in her chest reminded her to draw in a breath but despite the fact she obeyed her body's demand to refill her lungs, the pain of betrayal by her best friend—the woman she loved like a sister—still lingered. How *could* Anna have known what was going to happen and not given her prior warning?

In her bag, her phone began to chirp insistently. Thinking it might be the taxi company calling back to confirm her details, she lifted it to her ear and answered it.

"Nicole, where are you? Are you okay?"

Anna. Who else? It certainly wouldn't be her father calling to see if she was all right.

"I'm fine," Nicole answered, her voice clipped.

"You're not fine, you're upset. I can hear it in your voice. Look, I'm sorry about tonight—"

"Just tonight, Anna? What about your trip to Adelaide? What about bringing my brother home for the first time in twenty-five years, so he could take everything that was ever mine away from me?" Even Anna's gasp of pain at Nicole's accusations didn't stop Nicole's tirade or do anything to lessen the hurt of betrayal that rocketed through her veins right now. "I thought we were friends, sisters by *choice,* remember?"

"I couldn't tell you what Charles had planned, Nicole. Please believe me. Your dad swore me to secrecy and I owe him so very much. Without his support of me and my mum…you know what he was like…even when she was dying—"

"His support, huh?" Nicole shut her eyes tight and squeezed back the fresh round of tears that fought to escape. "What about your support of me?"

"You always have that, Nic, you know that."

"Really? Then why didn't you give me a heads-up? Why didn't you tell me that he was going to bribe Judd to stay by giving him my home as well as the business?"

"Only half the business," Anna's voice came quietly over the line.

"A controlling share, Anna. That's the whole business as far as I'm concerned."

The shock of her father's announcement had been bad enough. Worse was the way he'd justified the decision to give everything to Judd instead of her. *Just you wait,* he had said, *you'll find some young man who'll sweep you off your feet and before I know it you will be married and raising a family. Wilson Wines will just be a hobby for you.* Years of hard work, of dedication and commitment to the business and to further her father's plans and dreams dismissed as just a *phase,* a passing fad. The thought of it made her blood boil.

"Dad made it quite clear where I stand in all this, and by aligning yourself with him, you've made it quite clear where you stand, too."

Nicole paced back and forth on the pavement at the end of the driveway, filled with a nervous energy that desperately needed an outlet. Anna's voice remained steady in her ear; the sound of her friend's voice was usually a calming influence but tonight it was anything but.

"He put me in an impossible position, Nic. I begged him to talk to you about this, to at least tell you that Judd would be coming home."

"Obviously you didn't beg hard enough. Or, here's something to consider, maybe you could have just told me, anyway. You could have picked up a phone or fired me an email in warning. It's not that hard to do. You had to know what this would mean to me, how much it would hurt me. And still you did nothing?"

"I'm so sorry, Nic. If I could do it over I'd do it differently, you have to know that."

"I don't know anything anymore, Anna. That's the trouble. Everything I've worked for, everything I've lived for, has just been handed to a man I don't even know. I don't even know if I have a roof over my head now that Dad's given the deed of the family house to Judd. How would that make *you* feel? Have you asked yourself that?"

A sweep of lights coming down the road heralded the taxi she'd summoned, and not a moment too soon. She had enough dander up right now to march back on up the driveway and give her father a piece of her mind all over again—for whatever good it would do.

"Look," she continued, "I've got to go. I need some space right now to think things over."

"Nicole, come back. Let's talk this out face-to-face."

"No," Nicole answered as the cab pulled up alongside the curb. "I'm done talking. Please don't call me again."

She disconnected the call and switched off her phone for good measure before throwing it into the bottom of her bag.

"Viaduct Basin," she instructed as she got into the taxi and settled in the darkened interior with her equally dark thoughts.

Hopefully the vibrant atmosphere at the array of bars and clubs in downtown Auckland would provide her with the distraction she needed. Nicole repaired her tear-stained makeup as well as she could with the limited cosmetics in her bag. It annoyed the heck out of her that anger, for her, usually resulted in tears, as well. It was an awkward combination that plagued her on the rare occasions she actually lost her temper, and it made it hard for her to be taken seriously.

She willed her hand to be steady as she applied a rich red lip gloss and gave herself a final check in her compact mirror.

Satisfied she'd done her best with her makeup, she sat back against the soft upholstery of the luxury taxi and tried to ignore the echo of her father's words, the faintly smug paternal tone that seemed to say that she'd soon get over her temper tantrum and realize he was right all along.

"Over my dead body," she muttered.

"Pardon, miss, what was that you said?" the neatly suited taxi driver asked over his shoulder.

"Nothing, sorry, just talking to myself."

She shook her head and blinked hard at the fresh tears that pricked in her eyes. In doing what her father had done he'd permanently damaged his relationship with her, fractured the trust between her and Anna, and virtually destroyed any chance of her and Judd building a sibling bond together. She had no family she could rely on anymore—not her father, her brother, her sister and certainly not her mother. Nicole had not seen or heard from her mother since Cynthia Masters-Wilson had taken Judd back to her native Australia when he was six and Nicole only one year old.

Nicole had long since convinced herself she'd never wanted to know her mother growing up. Her father had been everything and everyone she'd ever needed. But even as a child, she'd always been able to tell that she wasn't enough to make up for the wife and son that her father still missed. It had driven Nicole to work harder, to be a top student and to learn everything she could about the family business, in the hopes of winning her father's approval, making him proud. Goodness only knew running Wilson Wines was all she'd ever wanted to do from the moment she'd understood just what held the balance of her father's attention every day.

Now that Judd was back, it was as if she didn't exist anymore. As if she never had.

Nicole reached up to remove the hair tie that had held her hair in its no-nonsense, businesslike pony-tail all day, and shoved her fingers through her hair to tousle it out into party mode. She would not let her father's actions beat her. Once she'd worked this upset out of her system she'd figure out a way to fix things. Until then, she was going to enjoy herself.

She alighted from the taxi and paid the driver then undid the top button of her suit jacket, exposing a glimpse of the gold-and-black satin-and-lace bra she wore beneath it. There, she thought defiantly, from business woman to party girl in one easy step. Squaring her shoulders, Nicole headed into the first bar on the strip. Oblivion had never looked better.

Nate leaned against the bar and watched the pulsing throng of bodies on the dance floor with disinterest. He'd only agreed to come along tonight for Raoul's sake. Hosting the guy's stag party was small recompense for the work Raoul had done holding Jackson Importers together after Nate's father's sudden death last year. Knowing the running of the business was in Raoul's very capable hands until Nate could return to New Zealand to pick up the reins had been a massive relief. Extricating himself from Jackson Importers' European office and appointing a replacement there had taken time, and he owed the guy big for stepping up to the plate.

His philanthropy didn't assuage his boredom, however, and Nate was on the verge of saying his goodbyes and making his way home when she caught his eye. The woman moved on the dance floor with a sensuous grace that sent a spiraling swell of primal male interest through his body. She was dressed as if she'd come from the office, although he'd never seen any of his staff look that good in a suit. Her jacket was unbuttoned just enough to give a tantalizing view of creamy feminine swells of flesh supported by sexy black satin and gold lace, and while her skirt wasn't exactly short, her long legs and spiky heels certainly made it look that way.

He felt a familiar twinge in his groin. All of a sudden, heading out to his home on the ocean side of the Waitakere Ranges wasn't his top priority anymore—at least not immediately and, hopefully, not alone.

Nate cut through the throng of seething bodies to get nearer. There was something familiar about her but he couldn't place it immediately. Her long dark hair swung around her face as she moved to the beat of the music and he imagined it swinging in other areas, gliding over his body. Oh, yes, definitely gliding over his body—or even spread across the starkness of his Egyptian cotton sheets while he glided across hers. He clenched and unclenched his jaw as every cell in his body responded to the visual image.

He let the beat of the music infuse him and eased in beside her. "Hi, can I join in?" he asked with a smile.

"Sure," she replied, before flicking her hair from her face and exposing dark eyes a man could lose himself in, and a delectably red-painted mouth that was made for pure sin.

They danced awhile, their bodies moving in synchronicity—close, but not touching. The air between them was incendiary. Would they move in such unison alone together, too?

Another dancer jostled past, knocking her against his chest. His hands whipped up to steady her and she looked up into his eyes with a smile that started slowly before spreading wide.

"My hero," she said, with a wicked gleam in her dark eyes.

He found his mouth curving in response. "I can be whatever you want me to be," he said, bending his head slightly and putting his mouth to the shell of her ear.

She quivered in his arms. "Anything?"

"Anything."

"Thank you," she said, so softly he almost couldn't hear her over the noise around them. "I could do with a dose of *anything* right now."

She draped her arms over his shoulders, the fingers of one hand playing with his hair where it sat at the nape of his neck. Her touch did crazy things to him. Things that made him want to do nothing more than take her out of here and transport her to his home, his bed.

Nate wasn't into one-night stands. Aside from the fact his mother had drilled respect for women into him from an early age, he'd never been that kind of guy. Nate liked to plan, to calculate all the angles—spontaneity wasn't really his strong suit, especially in his private life. He knew how important it was to be cautious, to keep people at a distance until you were sure of their motives. But there was something about the girl in his arms that made him want to take a chance.

He looked down into her face and recognition began to dawn. Suddenly he knew why she'd seemed familiar. She was Nicole Wilson—none other than Charles Wilson's daughter, and the second in command at Wilson Wines. Her picture had been in the dossier of information he'd asked Raoul to gather on the competition's business—and most especially on the man who had once been his father, Thomas's, closest and oldest friend. Charles Wilson, who had—after an angry row, rife with false accusations—subsequently become Thomas's bitterest rival.

Once, when he'd been a turbulent teen, Nate had promised his father he'd seek revenge for what Charles Wilson had done. Thomas, ever the peacemaker, had told him he was to do no such thing while Thomas still drew breath. Sadly now, his father was dead—not so sadly, all bets, in relation to Charles Wilson, were off.

Nate wasn't normally one to deliver on the sins of the father, but tonight's potential now took on a whole other edge. He'd been biding his time with Charles Wilson. Accumulating information, and planning his strategy carefully. But even if it hadn't been part of his plans, he wasn't about to ignore the opportunity that had just dropped into his arms.

A waft of Nicole's fragrance drifted off her heated body and teased his nose. The scent was rich and spicy, very much, he suspected, like the woman he held— their bodies moving in unison, undulating to the beat of the music that thrummed around them.

Nate didn't hide the arousal he felt for her. What was the point? If this didn't work out, then there'd be no foul. His plans would carry on regardless. But if it did,

if she was responding to him the same way he reacted
to her, his plans for revenge against Charles Wilson
would take a very interesting turn indeed.

Nicole knew she'd had too much to drink tonight,
and she knew full well that she should call another taxi
to take her home. After all, it was only Thursday and
she still had work tomorrow. At least, she thought she
still had work tomorrow.

Thinking about work made her head hurt and the
idea of returning to the house tonight just tied her
stomach in knots and reminded her again of her father's low opinion of her. Earlier, she'd blocked out that
reminder with a shot, and then another, egged on by a
group of acquaintances she'd barely seen since she'd
graduated from university and whom she could hardly
call friends. Still, their lively and undemanding company tonight had been just what she sought. No questions, no answers. Just being lost in the moment. And
right at this moment she was feeling very lost indeed.
Lost in the undeniable attraction between two healthy
young people in their prime.

Very little separated her and her dance partner and
as her lower body brushed against him again, a classic
Mae West line ran through her alcohol-clouded mind.
She couldn't stifle the giggle that bubbled up from
inside.

"Care to share the joke?"

She pressed her lips together and shook her head.
There was no way she was sharing that little snippet.

"Then you have to pay a forfeit—you know that,
don't you?"

"A forfeit?" she asked, her lips spreading into a

smile once more. "Surely you can't punish a girl for being happy?"

"I wasn't thinking of a punishment," he said.

She should be laughing at the line he'd just uttered, she told herself, yet, for some reason, a wicked coil of lust tightened inside her.

"Oh?" she managed through lips that she suddenly felt the urge to moisten with the tip of her tongue. "What were you thinking of?"

"This," he said.

She didn't have time to think, or room to move had she even wanted to dodge him, as he lowered his lips to hers. Lips that were unexpectedly cool and firm. Lips that sampled, tasted and teased her own.

The tight sensation inside her spread, tingling through her body like a slow-building charge of electricity, sensitizing her hidden places, draining her mind of any awareness of her surroundings. All she could think of, all she *wanted* to think of, was the touch of his mouth on hers. Of the delicious pressure of his body as his hands on her hips gathered her closer.

They continued to move to the music—her pelvis rolling against his, her awareness of his arousal becoming a hunger for more than the illicit touch of bodies through clothing. A moan built deep in her throat, a moan she fought to keep inside as he lifted his mouth from hers.

She swallowed and opened her eyes. In this light it was difficult to tell what color his eyes were, but they were definitely unusual and their hooded stare captured her and held her mesmerized. Didn't certain beasts of prey do the same? Was she about to be devoured? The thought didn't upset her as much as it should. God, she had to pull herself together.

"So, that's a forfeit, huh?" she asked, her voice thick with desire.

"It's just one of many."

"Intriguing."

Intriguing wasn't the word. His kiss had totally fried her synapses. It was all she could do to prevent herself from dragging his face down to hers again and repeating the experience. Once more with feeling, she thought, although she certainly hadn't been devoid of feeling while he'd been kissing her. For that moment in time she'd forgotten everything. Who she was, why she was here, what she had left to look forward to.

She'd liked that. She'd liked it a whole lot. She wanted to do it again.

"Hey, Nic!"

One of her acquaintances, Amy, appeared at her side and her dance partner released her. She instantly rued the loss of contact.

Her friend shouted to be heard over the music. "We're off to another club, you coming?"

Nicole's usual prudence screamed "safety in numbers" at the back of her mind, but tonight she wasn't in the mood to be prudent at all.

"No, I'm fine. I'll get a taxi home later."

"Okay. Hey, it was cool catching up again. Let's not leave it so long next time."

And then Amy was gone with the crowd she'd been hanging with.

"Are you sure you didn't want to go with your friends?" her dance partner asked.

"No, I'm fine. I'm a big girl, I can look after myself," Nicole answered.

"I'm pleased to hear it. I'm Nate, by the way."

"Nicole," she answered shortly, happy to keep their

introductions brief as she threw herself back into the
thrum and energy of the DJ's latest sound selection.

She was distracted by the flash of someone's
camera, no doubt someone's shenanigans would be
broadcast on some social networking site tomorrow,
but before long her focus was solely on the man in front
of her. Boy, but he could move. Some guys just looked
as if they were trying too hard on the dance floor but
for him, movement came very naturally. And he was
so good to look at, too.

His hair was dark, but not as dark as her near-black
tresses, and his face was both masculine and had a re-
fined elegance at the same time. And those lips—she
was very keen for a repeat of what they had to offer.

"Do I pass muster?" he asked, one corner of his
mouth twisting upward.

She smiled in response. "You'll do."

He laughed and the sound went straight to her toes,
making them curl in delight. Was there anything about
him that wasn't gorgeous?

The crowd around them had begun to thin and
Nicole started to become aware that eventually this
night would have to end. At about that point she'd
be feeling the pain of dancing in high heels for several hours, along with the aftereffects of too much to
drink. She hated that reality had to intrude again, especially when she was having such a good time. Nate
said something, but over the frenetic pulse of the music
she didn't quite make it out.

"What was that you said?" Nicole asked, leaning
closer.

Mmm, he even smelled great—like a cool ocean
breeze.

"I said, would you like a drink?"

She'd probably had quite enough for one night but an imp of mischief prompted her to nod her head.

"Here? Or we could head back to my place if you'd rather."

She felt a frisson of excitement. Was he suggesting what she thought he was suggesting? She'd never done this before—gone back to some random guy's house for a drink, at least not without a posse of friends with her. But for some reason she felt as if she could trust Nate, and then there was that amazing energy between them. She deserved to find out if those sparks were real, didn't she? Wouldn't it be some solace for the night she'd put up with?

"Your place is fine."

Actually, anywhere but home was fine.

"Great." He smiled, the action sending a sizzle of anticipation thrilling through her veins.

Sore feet and the prospect of a hangover were the furthest things from her mind as Nate took her hand and led her toward the exit. And if thoughts of "danger" or "risk" occurred to her, she brushed them aside. Tonight was a night for taking chances.

And besides, what was the worst that could happen?

# Two

Nate caught Raoul's eye as he led Nicole away, giving his friend a nod. He briefly saw Raoul's answering wink before the expression on the other man's face changed to one of shocked recognition. Nate fought back the smug smile that pulled at his lips.

In all the years he'd spent imagining how he would bring Charles Wilson to his knees, he'd never once imagined this scenario. But then, he'd never imagined taking Charles Wilson's daughter in his arms and feeling such a searing sense of attraction, either. With such a ripe opportunity before him, he'd be a fool not to make the most of it—in every way possible. Still, he had to be careful. It wouldn't do to put the cart before the horse. He could just as easily be calling a taxi to take Nicole home after their drink, but something inside him told him that was very unlikely.

He reached in his pocket and pressed the remote to

the low-slung silver Maserati that waited for them at the curb.

"Very pretty car," Nicole commented as he held open the passenger door for her and she folded her delicious long legs into the passenger bay.

"I like to travel in style," he answered with a smile.

"I like that in a man," she answered, her lips curving in response.

He just bet she did. She'd never wanted for anything and every part of her life had been to the highest standard. It stood to reason that Nicole Wilson's demands of her men would be high. It was a gauntlet he relished picking up.

Unlike Nicole, Nate knew what it was like to struggle—his father had been a living example of the concept for most of Nate's childhood. After Charles Wilson had kicked him out of the business they'd built together, it had taken years for Thomas to reestablish his credibility and build a company of his own. Nate had watched as his father poured his everything into his fledgling business in an attempt to provide something, anything, to the woman he'd accidentally gotten pregnant and the son their liaison had borne. And while Thomas had done his best to shield his only child, the experience had left its mark, resulting in two rules that Nate had lived his life by ever since. Rule one: be very careful who you trust.

Rule two: all's fair in love and war.

Nate slid into the driver's seat and started the car, maneuvering it smoothly toward Hobson Street and the entrance to the North Western motorway.

"You're a Westie?" Nicole asked.

"After a fashion," he answered. "I have a couple of

places. Karekare is where I call home. You still want that drink at my place?"

His challenge hung between them in the dark interior of the car. He shot her a glance and saw her press her lips together and swallow before answering.

"I'm all good. I haven't been out to Karekare in ages."

"It's still pretty much the same. Wild and beautiful."

"Like you?" she asked, her eyes gleaming as she shot him a glance.

"I was thinking more along the lines of you."

She laughed, the sound filling the cabin of his car and making his gut tighten in anticipation.

"Oh, you're good. You know all the right things to say to salve a wounded soul."

"Wounded?" he probed.

"Just family stuff. Too complicated and too boring to bring up now," she hedged.

Was all no longer well in the Wilson household? Nate wondered. He'd made it his business to know what happened within Wilson Wines and he'd heard of the return of the prodigal son. Had Judd Wilson's arrival served to uplift the mantel of golden child off Nicole's shoulders?

"We have a long drive," Nate pointed out as they entered the motorway and his car picked up speed. "I'm willing to listen if you want to talk about it."

"Just the usual," she said with an attempt at flippancy. An attempt that failed judging by the tone of her voice.

"Sounds serious," he commented, keeping his eyes looking forward out the windscreen.

She sighed, the sound coming from somewhere deep

down inside her. "I had a fight with my dad. At the risk of sounding clichéd, he doesn't understand me."

"Isn't that a parental prerogative?"

She laughed, a short, sharp sound in total contrast to the last time she'd done so. "I suppose so. I just feel so used, you know? I have spent my whole life trying to measure up, to be the best daughter, the best workmate, the best—well, everything. And he thinks I should settle down and have *babies!* As if. You know, I think he values a paper clip on his desk more highly than he does me. I've spent the past five years helping him to keep our family business thriving and he tells me it's a nice *hobby* for me."

"I suppose this argument is what led you to the club tonight?"

"Too right it is. I couldn't stay under his roof another second. Oh, no, wait. It's not *his* roof anymore, nor mine. He's gone and given it all to my dear long-lost brother." She expelled an angry huff of air. "I'm sorry, I'm always letting my mouth run away with me. I shouldn't have said that. Just pretend you didn't hear that last bit, okay? I think we should change the subject. Talking about my family is just going to spoil my mood."

"Whatever the lady wants, the lady gets," Nate replied smoothly, even though his curiosity burned to know more about the Wilson family home situation.

"Now that's more like it." Nicole laughed in response. "A girl could get used to that attitude."

"What, you mean that isn't always the case?"

Nicole swiveled slightly in her seat and stared at him. "You say that as if you think you know me."

"You misunderstand me," he said smoothly. "I just

would have thought that a woman like you would have no trouble getting what she wanted."

She gave an inelegant snort, then change the subject. "Tell me about your home. Are you overlooking the beach?"

He nodded. Partly in concession to her change of subject and partly in answer to her question. "I'm on a slight rise looking out onto Union Bay."

"I've always loved the West Coast. The black sand beaches, the crazy surf. There's something so, I dunno, untamed, unpredictable about it all."

"You surf?"

She shook her head. "No, always been too chicken."

Somehow she didn't strike him as the type of woman to be afraid of anything, and he said as much.

"Some boundaries I just never pushed. I grew up as an only child with a parent who could be pretty strict. Sometimes my dad took overprotectiveness a little far."

"Only child? You mentioned a brother?"

"He lived with our mother up until recently. And how on earth did we get back on that awful topic again?"

She pushed a hand through her tangled long hair, exposing the sweep of her high cheekbones and the determined set of her jaw. His fingers itched to trace the fine bone structure, to taste the smooth skin that stretched over it. Nate tightened his grip once more, dragging his eyes back to the road and his mind back to the goal at hand. Yes, he wanted her. And yes, he had every intention of having her. But he couldn't let himself lose control. He had to keep the endgame in mind.

"What about you?" she asked, turning in her seat to look at him. "What's your family like?"

"Both my parents are gone. My mother while I was

in university, my dad more recently. I never had any brothers or sisters."

"So you're all alone? Lucky you." She gasped as if she realized the potentially pain-filled minefield she'd just trodden into. "I'm sorry, that was insensitive."

"No, it's okay. I miss them but I still count myself lucky to have had them both in my life. And my dad was a great role model. He worked his heart out, literally, to provide for us, and I got to repay that once I graduated and started working in the family firm."

Nate deliberately kept things vague. He wouldn't, for a moment, begin to elaborate on exactly why his father's health took such a beating as he strived to build a new business from the ground up. Or who was responsible for that.

"So, surfing?" he asked, very deliberately changing the subject as he took the exit he needed that would eventually lead them out toward the beach.

"What about it?"

"Want to try it over the weekend?"

"This weekend?"

"Sure, why not stay. I have spare boards, spare wetsuits."

"Spare clothes, underwear?" She gestured to her voluminous bag on the car floor. "It might be a big bag but it's hardly *Doctor Who's* TARDIS, you know."

Nate laughed. Her sharp wit was refreshing and appealing at the same time.

"Let's play it by ear then, hmm? Trust me?"

"Sure. If I didn't think I could trust you, I wouldn't be here."

He reached across and took her hand, caressing the soft skin of her inner wrist with his thumb.

"Good."

He let go and placed his fingers firmly back on the steering wheel. From the corner of his eye he saw that she stroked her wrist with the fingertips of her other hand. He allowed himself a small smile of satisfaction. This night was going perfectly.

So why *did* she trust him, she wondered as she lapsed into silence and looked idly out the passenger window. It's not as if she knew him. She'd acted purely on instinct, a fact that—despite her earlier assertion about being a chicken—had gotten her in trouble many a time before.

She gave herself a mental shake. She deserved this night. She had it coming to her after the crap she'd put up with at dinner on top of everything else this week. And everything in her body told her that this was the man to take all her problems away—at least for the night.

Her skin still tingled where he'd touched her, the sensation a delicious buzz of promise hovering just beneath the surface. Did he expect to make love to her tonight? Just the thought of it sent a thrill of longing through her body, making her womb clench tight on a swell of need that all but knocked the air from her lungs. She'd never had this intense a reaction to anyone before. Just sneaking a glance at his hands on the steering wheel, at the way his long fingers curled around the leather, made her want those fingers on her, in her. She pressed her thighs together and felt the swollen heated flesh at her core respond. Just thinking about him touching her was nearly enough to make her go off. What would it be like when he did?

She cleared her throat against the sudden anticipatory lump that lodged there.

"Everything okay?" Nate asked.

"Sure. It's quite a drive from the city to your place. Do you work in town?"

"Yeah. I keep an apartment there for the nights I'm too tired to make it back out to Karekare, or if I have an early run to the airport or early meetings. I sleep better with the sounds of the sea and the rainforest around me, though."

"Sounds idyllic."

"You'll see soon enough for yourself."

She fell silent as they entered Scenic Drive, letting her body sway with the roll of the car as they wound on the narrow ribbon of road higher into the ranges, before winding back down again on the other side. She must have dozed off a little because the next thing she knew the Maserati was driving up a steep incline and pulling into a well-lit garage. A glance at her watch said it was almost 2:00 a.m. The drive had taken nearly an hour. She was miles from anyone she knew, miles from home. She should find the fact daunting—she didn't. In fact, she welcomed it. Knew that with her choice to come home with Nate that she'd thrown her cares to the wind.

"Home sweet home," Nate said, coming around to her side of the car and opening the door for her.

Nicole accepted his hand as he helped her out the car, her senses purring at his touch. To her surprise he didn't let go, instead leading her to a doorway which, when opened, revealed a short set of stairs leading down into a massive open-plan living/dining and kitchen area.

The furnishings were comfortable but spoke plainly of their price in the elegantly simple designs and top-quality fabrics. A large, open fireplace, bordered with gray slate, occupied space on one wall. Even the art-works on the walls and small sculptures on the occa-sional shelving were beautiful and no doubt expensive. What he surrounded himself with said a lot about him and, so far, she liked it.

"Still feel like that drink?" Nate asked, lifting her hand to his lips and pressing a kiss against her knuck-les.

"Sure, what are we having?"

"There's champagne in the fridge, or we could have a liqueur."

"A liqueur, I think."

Something potent and heady, just like him, she thought privately. Nate let her hand go and moved toward a built-in sideboard on the other side of the room. She gravitated toward the wall of glass that faced the inky darkness outside. Beyond the floor-to-ceiling windows she could hear the sound of waves rolling heavily into shore.

In the reflection of the glass she saw Nate come to stand behind her, one arm coming around to offer her a small glass of golden liquid.

"A toast, I think," he said, his breath warm in her hair and making her scalp prickle in awareness.

"To what in particular?" Nicole asked, accepting her glass and raising it toward Nate's pale facsimile mir-rored before her.

"To wounded souls, and the healing of them."

She nodded and raised her glass to her lips, her taste buds reacting instantly to the smooth, sweet tang of aged malt whiskey. She allowed the liquid to stay on her tongue for a moment before swallowing.

"Now that is pretty fine," she said, turning to face Nate. Her breath caught in her chest as she saw the look in his eyes. Eyes that were only a shade darker than the deep gold fluid in their glasses.

"Only the best," he answered before closing the distance between their faces.

Nicole felt her heart race in her chest. If this kiss was to be anything like the one at the club she couldn't wait to experience it. Her lips parted expectantly, her gaze focused solely on the shape of his mouth, on the sheen left there by the liqueur. Her eyelids slid closed as she felt the warmth of him, as his lips took hers, as his tongue swept gently across the soft fullness of her lower lip.

He made a sound of appreciation. "Now that's what I call the best."

His lips pressed against hers once more and she curved into his body as one arm slid around her back and drew her closer to him. He was already aroused, a fact that triggered an insistent throb in her veins— a throb that went deeper into her center. She pressed her hips against him, feeling his length, his hardness. Feeling her body respond with heat and moisture and need.

She could taste the liqueur on his lips, on his tongue—its fusion of flavors intrinsically blended with his own. When he withdrew she felt herself move with him, toward him. Drawn as if by some magnetic force.

Nate put his liqueur glass on a shelf nearby before also taking hers and doing the same again. He then lifted his hands to her hair, pushing his fingers through the long mass until his fingertips massaged the back of her scalp, gently tilting her face to his once more. This time his kiss held a stronger taste of hunger, a promise of things to come.

Nicole tugged his shirt free of his waistband and

shoved her hands underneath, her nails gently scoring his back as she traced the line of his spine, up, then down. Logic tickled at the back of her mind a final time, telling her she shouldn't be here, shouldn't be doing this, but need and desire overcame logic with the same inexorable surge and release of the waves that echoed on the darkened shore outside.

He wanted her. She wanted him. It was basic and primal and it was all she needed for now. That, and a whole lot of satisfaction.

Nate's hand shifted to the buttons on her jacket, swiftly loosening them from their button holes and pushing aside the fabric, exposing her to him. His hands were broad and warm as they swept around the curve of her waist before skimming her rib cage and moving up toward her bra.

He released her lips, bending his head lower, along her jaw line, down the sensitive cord of her neck and across her collarbone. She felt her breasts grow heavy. Her nipples beading tight, almost painfully so, behind her expensive lace-covered satin bra. When the tip of his tongue swept across one creamy swell she shuddered in response, the sensation of the point of his tongue electric as it traced a fine line across the curve of one breast. He awarded the same attention to her other breast, this time sending a sharp spear straight to her core.

His tongue followed the edge of her bra before dipping in the valley between. Her breath came in quick pants, her heart continuing to race in her chest. She felt his hand at her back, felt the freedom of the clasp of her bra being released, the weight of her breasts falling free as he slid her jacket off her shoulders and pushed her bra straps down to follow. With scant regard for the designer labels of both garments, Nate let them drop to the polished timber floor.

Nicole was beyond caring as his mouth captured one extended nipple, pulling it gently between his teeth, laving it with the heat of his tongue. Her legs began to tremble and she clung to him, near mindless with the pleasure his touch brought her. When his hands went to the waistband of her skirt she barely noticed, and then, with a slither of silk lining, her skirt joined her bra and jacket on the floor at her feet.

Dressed only in a scanty pair of black-and-gold panties and her high-heeled, black patent pumps she should have felt vulnerable, but as Nate pulled away, his eyes caressing every inch of her, she felt powerful. Needed. Wanted.

"Tell me what you want," he demanded, his voice a low demand that vibrated across the space between them.

"I want you to touch me," she replied softly.

"Show me where."

She lifted her hands to her bare breasts, her fingers cupping their smooth fullness, lifting them slightly before her fingertips abraded the distended tips, sending another shudder through her.

"Here," she said, her voice thicker now.

"And?"

One hand crept down, over her flat belly, and to the top band of her panties.

"Here." Her voice trembled as she felt the heat that pooled between her legs, felt the moisture that awaited his touch, his possession.

"Show me what you like," he said, his hand sliding over hers.

"This," she replied, letting their hands push beneath the scrap of fabric.

She led his fingers toward her opening, dipping them in her wetness before sliding them back up toward the budded bundle of nerves that screamed for his touch. She circled the sensitive spot first with her fingers then with his, increasing the pressure then slowing things down before repeating the cycle once more.

"Keep touching yourself," he commanded, even as he slid his fingers out from beneath her hand, dipping them lower until they played within the soft folds of her flesh.

He hooked his other arm around her, supporting her weight as he stepped in a little closer. She felt the fabric of his trousers against her bare legs—a fleeting awareness only before all concentration went when he stroked one finger inside her body, then another. Her muscles clenched against him as his fingertips glided in and out, caressing with careful and deliberate pressure against her inner walls.

Sensation swirled throughout her body, drenching her with heat and pleasure. The combination of both their touches filled her with an overpowering awareness of him, his strength, his power over her. She'd never felt anything this deep, this intense. Had never been this reckless.

Nate bent slightly, capturing one nipple with his mouth, drawing the sensitive bud into his heat, his wetness, and suckling hard. As he did so, she felt the pressure of his fingers inside her increase and with that subtle change, her body splintered apart on a wave of satisfaction so intense, so immeasurable, that her legs

buckled beneath her and tiny pin pricks of light danced
behind her eyelids.

Her whole body shook with the intensity of her
orgasm as ripple after ripple of pleasure coursed
through her. She felt Nate withdraw from inside her,
even as her inner muscles continued to pull and tighten
against him, heightening the sensations and sending
her into another short, sharp paroxysm of bliss. He slid
one hand behind her knees and, with his other arm still
supporting her back, he swept her into his arms and
strode across the open plan area toward a darkened
room.

His bedroom, her shattered senses finally recognized as he placed her on the bedcovers. In the fractured blend of moon and starlight that shone through
the massive picture window, she watched as he stripped
away his clothing. Exposing every inch of his silver-
gilded male beauty to her gaze. He reached for her
feet, removing the shoes she only just now realized
she still wore, then his hands slid up the length of her
legs. When he reached her panties he slowly removed
them from her before lowering himself to the bed and
gently kneeing her legs apart, settling between them.

He leaned across her and ripped open a bedside cabinet drawer and removed a box of condoms. Extract-
ing a packet he made short work of ripping away the
wrapper and rolling the protection over his jutting erection. Her hands fluttered to the breadth of his shoulders, his skin burning beneath her touch. Despite his
clear and evident arousal, his movements were smooth,
controlled and deliberate as he positioned himself at
her entrance and looked up to meet her eyes, even now
giving her the chance to change her mind, to decide for

herself what she wanted. In response, she instinctively tilted her pelvis to welcome his invasion.

Nate lowered his face to hers, his lips a heated seal against her own, his tongue gently probing her mouth even as he eased his length within her. She felt her body stretch to accommodate his size, felt an unmistakable quiver deep inside. Nicole lifted her hands to his head, her fingers lacing through his hair as she held him to her and kissed him back with all she had left in her.

Her body swept to aching life as he began to move, his thrusts powerful and deep, so deep it felt as if he touched her very soul before she plunged into the abyss of sensual gratification once more. In answer, his body stiffened, buried to the hilt, and a nearly stifled cry of release broke from him as he gave over to his own climax, shuddering as her body clenched rhythmically around him. His lips found hers again as he settled his weight on top of her, and she welcomed him. It was real, he was real. His heart thudded in his chest and hers beat a rapid tattoo in answer.

What they'd done together was something unsurpassed in her experience and finally, as she drifted to sleep, the cares and worries of her life wafted away into oblivion.

# Three

As Nate woke, he slowly became aware that he'd fallen asleep not just on top of Nicole, but still inside her, as well. He silently castigated himself for his inconsiderate behavior as he carefully supported his weight without waking her.

He ignored the unfamiliar urge to settle closer to her rather than pulling away. After all, certain precautions had to be observed, he reminded himself. He reached between them, feeling for the edge of his condom and cursing when he couldn't find it. He pulled farther away from her, his body instantly lamenting the lack of contact with her lush warmth. The condom was still inside her. In a moment of panic he wondered if she was on the Pill but that fear was quickly assuaged. A woman like Nicole wasn't the type to leave things to chance. It was highly unlikely that pregnancy was something either of them needed to worry about just now.

No, now was a time to concentrate on pleasure. They'd had sex once and he couldn't wait to repeat the experience.

He eased his hand between her splayed legs and found the condom, removing it carefully before disposing of it in his bathroom. As he eased his body back onto the bed beside her he safeguarded them once more by rolling on another sheath and gathered her to him. She curled instinctively against his body, her softness pressing against the hard muscled planes of his chest, her inner heat already beckoning to him.

Her eyes flickered open, a slow smile spreading across her face. He cupped one cheek in his hand. It was one thing to know from Raoul's report that Nicole Wilson was an attractive woman with an incredibly sharp business mind, but it was quite another to discover that she was also a warm and generous lover. The knowledge skewed his vision of how this would ultimately play out.

Sending Nicole back to her father was no longer an option. With a little luck, her anger against her father and her brother just might be deep enough and strong enough to make her willingly defect to Jackson Importers…and to Nate's bed. With Nicole at his side he could take Jackson Importers to the ultimate heights of success, while ensuring his nights were equally, if not more, satisfying.

Of course, there was always the possibility that loyalty to her family would win out. Nate would be a fool not to plan for that contingency. If that happened, he'd have to be more…creative in the methods he used to keep Nicole. He didn't want to hurt her—Charles was his only target—but if upsetting her a little was the price to get his revenge *and* keep Nicole in the bargain, then that was a price he was willing to pay.

Sooner or later, she'd thank him for it. He'd already known her father hadn't utilized her intelligence to his best advantage. But Nate would. And she'd know she was appreciated while he did it. Every glorious inch of her.

"You're so beautiful," he said, meaning every syllable.

"It's dark," she replied, a teasing note in her voice. "Everyone is beautiful in the dark. You can't see their bad side."

"You don't have a bad side," he said, leaning forward to kiss her.

"Everyone has a bad side, Nate. We just don't always show it."

There was a painful truth in her words. A truth he knew related directly to him and his intentions but he didn't want to think about that right now. More pressing matters were most definitely at hand.

"Sometimes it's better not to see, then, isn't it?" he asked before leaning across the short distance between them and kissing her.

Their lips touched in a burst of heat and desire, his every nerve striving to attain the heights of fulfillment he knew he would reach in her arms. This time the fire inside him burned steadily, not threatening to overwhelm him as it had before, but his hunger for her had not lessened despite the change in his appetite. This was to be savored, slowly, completely.

Time faded into obscurity and nothing mattered right now except the giving and receiving of pleasure. Each touch destined to bring a sigh or a moan from its recipient, each kiss a seal of the promise of what was yet to come. And when she positioned herself over his body and lowered herself over his straining flesh he gave himself over totally to her demands.

Their peak was no less intense than that first time together, and this time, when Nicole fell into his arms lost in the aftermath and falling rapidly into sleep, he made certain the same accident with the condom didn't occur a second time.

The next time he woke, sunlight was filtering through the native bush outside and into his bedroom window. He reached across the bed. Empty. Where was his quarry now, he wondered as he swung his legs over the side of the bed and stood, stretching as he did so.

"Nice view," a voice said from behind him.

He turned slowly, a smile on his face. A smile that widened when he saw that Nicole had found the camcorder he kept for filming some of the more wild surfing antics on the beach.

"Do you have a license to drive that thing?" he asked.

"I'm the kind of girl who likes to learn as she goes along," Nicole answered in response.

She was wearing just the shirt he'd worn last night, the fine cotton covering her body but leaving her long legs exposed to his hungry gaze.

"So you're more of the hands-on kind?" he said, feeling his body stir and his blood pump just a little faster.

"Oh, yes, definitely hands-on," she said, her voice a little rough around the edges.

"I've always thought practical experience to be vastly underrated, haven't you?" He was fully hard now. Every cell in his body attuned to her, to the camcorder she held, to the idea that now blossomed in his mind.

"Definitely underrated. And the value of visual aids, too."

Oh, God, he thought. She had just read his mind. "I have a tripod for that thing, you know."

She laughed, a deep throaty chuckle that made him clench his hands at his sides to stop himself from reaching for her.

"More than one, I'd say," she said, dropping the lens of the camera down, then slowly back up again to his face.

She was wicked. He liked that in a woman. He liked that a whole lot. "I'll go get the other one," he said with a slow wink.

Before she could say another word he brushed past her, dropping a kiss on the curve of her lips as he went by. "Why don't you get yourself comfortable on the bed? I'll be back in just a minute."

It took less than a minute before he was back in the bedroom and setting up the stand diagonal to the bed. She passed him the camera, her cheeks flushed with color, her eyes bright with anticipation. Beneath the fabric of his shirt he could see the sway of her breasts as she moved on the bed, not to mention the sharp peaks of her nipples that told of her excitement. She passed the camera to him and he carefully positioned it on its mount, ensuring the whole bed was square in the frame.

"You're sure about this?" he asked.

"Oh, very sure. And later, when we review it, we can see where we can improve."

He didn't think it was possible to get any harder but at that moment he did. It was one thing to know they were videoing themselves, another to know she wanted to watch it later.

"Where do you suggest we begin?" he asked, fighting to keep a lid on the carnal urge to simply have at her, to let her have at him and to hell with finesse.

"I think I need to get to know you better, don't you?" She patted the edge of the bed beside her. "Why don't you sit down?"

He sat and watched her as she slid off the tumbled linens and knelt between his legs on the rug beside the bed, placing her hands on the outside edges of his thighs, scratching lightly with her fingernails.

"It seems to me," she continued, "that last night was all about me. So this time, it's going to be all about you."

A fine tremor ran through his body and he watched as her hands stroked up his thighs and down again, each time working a little closer to the inside.

"Do you like that?" she asked.

He was beyond words and merely nodded.

"How about this?"

His mind nearly exploded as she bent her head and flicked the tip of her tongue over the aching head of his arousal. His penis jumped in response to her touch, a bead of moisture appearing only to be licked away just as quickly. Nicole's hair brushed against his inner thighs, obscuring her face. He reached down and pushed her hair aside, holding it against the back of her head with each fisted hand. He wanted to see this, all of it. And, just in case, he wanted the camera to see it, too.

Nicole felt an unaccustomed sense of possession as she lightly stroked her tongue along the length of

Nate's erection, painstakingly following the line of each vein from tip to base and back again. Heat rolled off him in waves as she did so and she felt him tremble as he fought to maintain control. But that control shattered the instant she took him fully in her mouth. He groaned, a guttural sound that came from deep in his belly, and she knew the exact moment he was going to climax. She increased the pressure of her mouth, her tongue, increased the rhythm of her movements until he spent himself. She slowed her pace, taking the last drop of his essence as he groaned again, his hands falling to his sides and his body falling back onto the bed behind him.

She pushed herself up onto the bed and lay propped on one elbow alongside him, letting her fingers trail up and down across his belly and chest as he caught his breath once more. His recovery said a whole lot about his fitness and stamina, she thought as he reached one arm up to her and dragged her down to kiss him. Already he was stirring again, and the knowledge gave her a wonderful feeling. It was all because of her.

"Mmm," she said, her lips bare centimeters from his. "Must be time for breakfast."

"Not yet," he said. "I think we should work up a bit more of an appetite first. And I think you should take that shirt off, too."

He deftly flicked open each button and slid one hand inside, cupping one breast and flicking his thumb across its hardened crest.

"I'm very hungry already," she purred. "I may take some convincing."

"You want convincing? I can be convincing," he said, pushing the shirt off her shoulders and then pressing her onto the bed.

What followed was an education in how someone could deliver a lifetime of hedonistic delight in very short order. Nate applied himself to her with assiduous intent, showing her just how artful he could be with the merest accessories—the tip of a tongue, a feather of breath, the stroke of a fingertip.

She was on the verge of begging, no, screaming for release when he finally sheathed himself with a condom and took them both over the edge of sanity and into a realm where only blithe elation resided.

The camera caught it all.

Their morning set the tone for the next three days. From time to time they would rise, bathe or eat—once taking a long stroll along the beach, Nicole wearing ill-fitting borrowed clothes—before the draw of their fascination with one another would take them back to bed again. By Monday morning Nicole was spent. Physically and emotionally, happy just to curl up against the hard male body beside her and revel in the intimacies they'd shared. Last night Nate had burned a DVD of their video and they'd viewed it while attempting to eat a civilized meal in the main room of the house.

The clothing they'd only recently donned—him in a pair of jeans and T-shirt, her in a sweatshirt of his with the sleeves rolled up and its length skimming the back of her thighs—had soon hit the floor. Their food cooling on their plates as the on-screen activity had incited a new hunger for one another all over again.

Nate still slept beside her and she watched his chest rise and fall on each breath. She was amazed at how natural it felt to be with him, especially considering how little they actually knew about one another. She'd heard the girls at work talk and giggle over their occasional one-night stands—guys they never expected, or in some cases even wanted, to see again—but she'd never believed she'd indulge in something quite so illicit herself. She felt as if the past few days had been a vacation, not just from work and responsibility, but from herself—her own fears and anxieties. On Friday she hadn't even given a care to the fact she had probably still been expected at the office, nor that over the course of the whole weekend she hadn't so much as told anyone where she was, nor checked her cell phone for messages.

It wasn't as if they cared, anyway, a little voice said from deep down inside. Her father didn't believe she had a valid contribution to make to the company, her best friend had turned on her and her brother? Well, he didn't even know her, nor she him. So what difference would it make if she walked away from all of them for good?

A whole lot of difference, she realized. She'd been angry on Thursday night. Really angry. And she'd acted completely out of character. Deep down she knew her family, including Anna, loved her and had to be worried about her having been out of touch for so long.

This person in the bed with a stranger, that wasn't her. Sure, it had been a great time, but all good things had to come to an end sometime, didn't they? Nothing this good ever lasted for long.

A wave of guilt for her behavior swamped her, driving her from the bed and into the bathroom where she gave in to the sudden well of tears in her eyes. She'd behaved irrationally. Stupidly. She had no idea of who she was really with. Everything that had anchored her these past twenty-six years lay on the other side of town—with her family, in her home. So what if her father had signed the property over to Judd? Her brother wasn't about to summarily eject her from the only home she'd ever known, surely. Judd was as much a victim of her father's shenanigans as she. So was Anna, who was far too grateful for all that Charles had done for her and her mother to ever tell him no.

And as for her father... It would be difficult for her to forgive or forget his words on Thursday night. But she couldn't forget twenty-six years of him sheltering and protecting her, either. For better or for worse, he was still her father. They'd just have to find a way to reach an accord. She was willing to take the first step, and come back home.

Nicole dashed her face with water and dried it before quietly letting herself out of the master bathroom and padding quietly across the bedroom floor. As she closed the door behind her she let go the breath she hadn't realized she'd been holding. She gave herself a mental shake. For goodness sake, she was an adult. Her decisions were her own, her choices were her own. The weekend had been great, just what she'd needed, there was no need to sneak around like a thief in the night.

She squared her shoulders and made her way to the laundry room where she'd hand washed and hung her underwear to dry during the course of the weekend. Her suit was on a hanger and had been brushed and steamed to get the creases out after being summarily left on the living room floor for several hours after Thursday night. She slid into her underwear and put on her suit. It felt strange to be dressed so formally after a weekend where clothing had been minimal.

She picked up her bag from in the living room and brushed out her hair before heading back to the bedroom to retrieve her shoes. She'd have to call a cab to get herself into work, she thought as she twisted her hair up into a knot and secured it with a clip she'd found in the bottom of her bag.

Nate was awake when she pushed open the door.

"Going somewhere?" he asked, his eyes unreadable as he watched her slide her feet into her shoes.

"Yeah, time to get back to reality." She sighed. "This weekend has been great. Better than great, thanks."

"That's it?"

"What—" she laughed nervously "—you want more?"

"I always want more, especially of what we've had."

"I never said I didn't want to see you again."

"But you implied it."

Nicole shot him a nervous glance. Was he going to get all weird on her now?

"Look, I need to get home and then head into work."

"No."

She shot him another look, this time the curl of fear in her stomach unfurled to bigger proportions.

"What do you mean, no?"

"What I mean is, you're coming to work with me."

Nate pushed aside the bed sheets and rose to his feet, calmly picking up the jeans he'd discarded last night and sliding them on. Nicole struggled to avert her gaze from the fine arrow of hair that angled down from his belly button to behind the waistband of his pants. She'd followed that path, and more, several times this weekend. A hot flush of color rushed to her cheeks. She couldn't let herself get distracted by sexual attraction. What on earth did he mean when he said she'd be working with him? She didn't even know what he did for a living. And he didn't know anything about her... did he?

"You've got it wrong, I have a job. A job I love, with a family I—"

"Don't tell me you love them, Nicole. Not after what they've done to you."

Instantly she rued the way she'd mouthed off in the car when he'd brought her here, and the truths she'd shared over a bottle of red wine as they'd curled naked beneath a blanket on the couch in front of a burning fire, late on Saturday night.

"They're still family. At the very least I need to clear the air with them."

"Oh, I think that's a bit more than they deserve. Besides, the air will clear soon enough."

Nicole crossed her arms across her stomach. "What on earth are you talking about?"

"When they learn who you've just spent this past weekend with, I very much doubt they'll be welcoming you home with open arms. I'm pretty much persona non grata with your father."

Nate's lips lifted in a half smile, as if he was laughing at a private joke.

"You're speaking in riddles. Why should they care who I spent the weekend with?" she snapped.

Nate came to stand in front of her. "Because I'm Nate Hunter—Nate Hunter Jackson."

Nicole's mind reeled on his words. Nate Hunter? *The* Nate Hunter? The reclusive billionaire who was the new head of Jackson Importers, her family firm's arch nemesis? Her father had never had a kind word to say about Thomas Jackson, or his staff.

Hang on a minute. Nicole replayed his words in her mind. Had he said Nate Hunter *Jackson?*

"I see you've made the connection," Nate said coolly. "And, yes, I am Thomas Jackson's son. Sweet, isn't it? All that time your father accused my dad of screwing around with your mother, he was actually with mine."

Nicole looked at him in horror as his words slowly sank in, leaving her mind reeling. She hadn't just been sleeping with a stranger over the entire weekend— she'd literally been sleeping with the enemy!

# Four

Nate watched the shock and dismay play across Nicole's features as understanding clouded her beautiful brown eyes.

"So you knew who I was all along? This weekend has all been about you getting some twisted revenge on my family?" she asked. Her voice shook, betraying just how much his words had upset her.

It might have started that way, Nate admitted to himself, but now he'd been with Nicole so intimately he knew that for the better part of their time together, revenge had been the last thing on his mind. At least, revenge on *her*. Her father, of course, was another matter entirely.

"Did you hunt me out?" she demanded, her voice stronger now.

"Our meeting was by chance," he said smoothly. "A happy chance from my point of view." He stepped forward and reached one finger to her cheekbone, tracing the smooth feminine contour to the corner of her lips. "And I don't regret a second of it, Nicole."

She jerked her head away. "Of course you don't," she said angrily. "Well, your little game is over now. I'm heading back into the city to my family and my job."

"I don't think so," Nate responded smoothly, crossing his arms in front of him.

"You can't possibly be serious about me working for you."

"I'm serious, all right."

"No." Nicole took a step back from him, putting one hand out as if she could physically prevent his words from holding any truth. "There's no way in this lifetime that I'd do such a thing, even if my father didn't want me at Wilson Wines. It would destroy every last vestige of our relationship together. He may not understand me as well as I'd hoped for, but he's still my father. I won't do that to him. I just won't."

Why couldn't she have stayed angry at her family? That would have made this so much easier, Nate thought to himself. Was there any way he could stoke that anger again?

"You *are* talking about the man who said that Wilson Wines was a nice hobby for you, aren't you?"

She shook her head, more in frustration, he imagined, than to negate what he'd just said. Nate pursued his advantage in the face of her silence.

"And you're talking about the man who, without a word of discussion with you—his right hand at Wilson Wines—gave away a controlling interest in his business to someone who is essentially a complete and utter stranger to both of you."

"Stop," she moaned, wrapping her arms about herself and holding them tight. "I know that's what he's done, you don't need to repeat it. He's my father. No matter what, he'll always be my dad. I'll always be loyal to him."

"Really? Why? He's even given away your family home, Nicole. Again, without any prior warning to you, nor any assurance for you that you will have a roof over your head anymore. Haven't you asked yourself yet what kind of man would do that to his daughter?"

Nate was angry, furiously angry. Not at Nicole, who seemed determined to forgive her father anything, but at the man who was at the root of all Nate's unhappiness. The man whose brutal rejection of his best friend had crushed Thomas Jackson's spirit and had forced him into dire financial straits. And the man who had withheld his encouragement and support from his daughter for so long that she'd forgive any insult for the chance to earn his approval.

He pressed on as she stood there silent and pale.

"You deserve more, Nicole. You deserve so much more. You're a strong, intelligent and incredibly capable woman. You should work somewhere where you're valued and appreciated. Think about the team we'll make. We'll be the best the business has ever seen."

She raised tear-washed eyes to his face and he fought to ignore the spear of regret that penetrated somewhere in the region of his chest. He knew his words hurt her but he couldn't afford to be soft, not now. If she didn't give in soon, he'd have to hurt her a lot more. He didn't want to, but he would, if it came to that. All was fair in love and war. And this was war.

"Nicole, your loyalty to Charles Wilson is commendable, but sadly misplaced. Work with me. Help me grow Jackson Importers to its fullest potential. Be a part of something special."

She swallowed before speaking. "And what's in it for you? You can't expect me to believe you're doing this out of the goodness of your heart."

He laughed, a short humorless sound that hung in the air between them for only a second or two. "No, I'm not doing it out of the goodness of my heart. I'm a businessman. I play to win, at all times and," he hesitated a moment for effect, "at all costs."

She shook her head again. "I won't work for you and I'm leaving right now. You're not the man I thought you were, Nate. I can't do what you're asking of me."

"Nicole, I'm not asking."

"I still have some say in this, don't I?" she demanded, turning and heading for the front door.

"Sure, you still have a say," he said, his words halting her in her tracks. "But so do I, and there's still a card left for me to play."

"I wasn't aware this was a game," she said coolly.

"Not a game at all," Nate said, smiling, even though his voice held no warmth anymore. "But all the same, I *will* win." He gestured toward the video camera still on the tripod in the corner of the room. "Ask yourself this, how would your father feel if he saw our amateur movie? What would hurt him more? Seeing you work for me, or knowing that you'd spent this past weekend in my bed?"

"Th—that's not fair," Nicole stammered, struggling to keep her balance. It felt as if the floor had been knocked out from under her. "I didn't know who you were then."

"I never said I play fair, Nicole. Your father already

hates the Jackson name. Already believes your mother slept with my father—it's what tore Charles and Thomas's friendship apart, what divided your family and what destroyed mine. I'll be sure to include a note with the DVD, explaining my parentage. How do you think he'd feel about seeing his daughter intimately engaged with Thomas Jackson's son?"

"You wouldn't!" Nicole uttered the words even though her throat felt as if it had constricted with shock and fear.

"Oh, believe me. I very much would. I want you, Nicole. I want you in my boardroom, in my office, in the field as well as here—in my home and in my bed."

Her skin tautened as his words fell upon her ears. Her nipples hardening even as a rush of warmth spread through her lower belly and her inner muscles clenched involuntarily in reaction to his words. Stop it, she told herself. He wasn't simply talking about sex. He was talking about her betraying her father. About her walking away from the company she'd hoped all her life that she would eventually take over. The job that was so much more than a job. It had been her way of life— her dream. It had been everything to her father and, ergo, everything to her, as well.

What Nate was suggesting was appalling. If she quit her job at Wilson Wines to work for Nate, her father would never understand, never forgive her. But could she take the risk that Nate would follow through on his threat and send her father a copy of their illicit weekend? Even as the thought presented itself in her mind, she knew without a shadow of a doubt that Nate would do exactly what he said. Men like him didn't always play fair or clean—and they rarely bluffed. It would

hurt her father if she worked for Nate but it would probably kill him if he saw that video.

"You're a bastard," she said quietly.

"Oh, yes, no question about that," Nate answered, a
thread of bitterness in his voice that she hadn't heard
before.

She racked her memory. Her father had rarely
spoken about the man who had been his best friend
from school, but when he did it had been in scathing
terms. Thomas Jackson had never married. Never even
publicly acknowledged he had a son. Was Nate even
telling the truth about his relationship with the man?

She was hit with a sudden wave of hopelessness. Did
any of her conjecture even matter when right now Nate
held all the cards very firmly in those dexterous hands
of his? Hands that had done wickedly delicious things
to her over the past seventy-two hours. She clamped
down on the thought before it took her over again. She
had to forget the man she thought she'd grown to know
a little these past few days. Had to remember, instead,
the hardheaded businessman who had so mercilessly
embarked on their time together knowing full well who
she was and what being with him would mean to her
family.

Her family. They were what had gotten her into this
mess. Them and her blasted impulsiveness. She could
see the lines of disappointment carved into her father's
face even now.

"So, Nicole, what's it to be?"

Nate stood opposite her, his hands loosely on his
lean jean-clad hips, his chest still bare, his shoulders
still showing evidence of their passion where she'd
clutched him tightly—her nails imbedding in his skin,
lost in the throes of yet more pleasure. Even now, with

his intentions out in the open, she still had to fight her desire for him. What did that say about her? She didn't even want to begin to examine that question.

She couldn't do it. She couldn't let her father see her wanton behavior, especially with the man who epitomized everything her father had fought against in the past twenty-five years. She had no other choice. She had to do as he said.

"You win."

"There, that wasn't too difficult, was it?"

She flung a fulminating look at him. "You have no idea."

She was damned if she did as he'd demanded, and she was damned if she didn't. At least this way she could protect her father from seeing the full extent of her own stupid behavior. Her face burned with shame as she remembered that she had been the one to pull out the camcorder in the first place. Furious and embarrassed, she pushed the thought away.

Nate Hunter Jackson might have won this round but he wouldn't win them all, she silently vowed. One way or another, she'd get her own back on him.

"This doesn't have to be a bad thing. At least with me you won't be taken for granted, Nicole," he said.

She ignored him. Being taken for granted was the least of her immediate worries. "I need to go home and get my things, and pick up my car," she said with as much control as she could muster.

"That won't be necessary."

She gestured to the suit she'd put back on this morning. Despite her attentions to it, the garment still looked a little the worse for wear and in need of a professional dry clean.

"Sorry to disappoint you, but I need my clothes. I can't wear this forever."

"Personally, I kind of like the idea of you not wearing it."

"Personally, I don't care what you like," she retaliated. She may have been forced into agreeing to his terms but she'd take a long walk off a short pier before she'd take her clothes off again at his behest. "I need my things—my car, my cell phone charger, everything. And I'll need to tell my father and brother that I won't be working for them anymore."

"I'll arrange for your car to be collected. As to your clothes, we can take care of that on the way into work. And, as to your father and brother, I'll take care of letting them know. There's no way to break it to them gently, and being blunt would be a miserable experience for you, but will be quite a lot of fun for me. Now, give me five minutes to shower and change. We can have breakfast in the city before we shop."

He turned and headed for the bathroom.

"I'm not hungry," she said to his retreating back.

Nate stopped and turned around, his hands already at the button fly of his jeans and exposing his lower abdomen to her gaze. "Not hungry? That's a shame. I'll have to have enough appetite for the both of us, then, won't I?"

Nicole dragged her eyes from the half open fly of his jeans and up to his face. His eyes burned with a heat that sent an answering response coursing through her body.

"Yes, you will," she said through teeth clenched so tight her jaw ached. She forced herself to relax the tiniest bit before continuing. "Because I have absolutely no appetite at all."

There, she thought, take that. She spun on one high heel and stomped through to the massive picture window facing the sea in the living room. Even there she was destined for disappointment, she thought. Instead of the rough roiling ocean she'd come to expect from the wild west coast beach ahead of her, there was nothing but a clear-blue autumn sky, rolling deep green water and foaming white crests of waves caressing the sparkling black sand shoreline. It was a complete contrast to the storm of emotion that tossed around inside her.

She was going to work for the son of her father's biggest business rival. He'd never forgive her this. Not in a million years. She shouldn't care, she told herself. He was the one who had summarily dismissed all her years of hard work for Wilson Wines and along with that dismissal had put aside her business and marketing degrees, not to mention the years of after-school and school holiday work experience she'd doggedly labored through so she could understand his business from the ground up. He'd never realized how important the business was to her because he'd never grasped how important *he* was to her.

Somewhere along the line, and from a very early age, Nicole had understood that her father's business was his everything. It was what he poured his heart and soul into every waking hour of every day. She'd thought that if she did exactly what he did, she'd earn his respect. And still he thought it was no more than a dalliance for her. Something to fill in her time before the more important matters of marriage and making babies filled her life.

Her hands tightened into fists, her perfectly manicured nails biting into the skin of her palms, as all her latent frustration built deep inside her. Getting angry at her father all over again would make it easier to walk away from Wilson Wines...but deep down, she knew the anger wouldn't last. She loved her father, and she knew that he loved her, even if they'd both fallen short on finding a way to connect. But even now, she refused to believe that it was too late. She closed her eyes to the perfection of the view outside and forced herself to draw in a steadying breath, and then another. Somehow she'd work her way through this. Somehow she'd work her way back to her family again.

"You ready?"

Nate's voice came from behind her. She opened her eyes and turned around. In a tailored charcoal-gray suit, with a crisp white shirt and flame-colored silk tie, he was a world away from the sensual creature who'd filled her weekend with sybaritic delight. A world away, but no less appealing. She ruthlessly pushed aside the admission.

"I was waiting for you, remember?" she said, scathingly.

He smiled, the action making something inside her tug hard. She silently cursed him for having this effect on her.

"Let's go, then."

The drive into the city was interminable. Nicole checked her cell phone for about the sixteenth time since they'd started out on the road. She hadn't had her phone on all weekend but even now the thing was down to only one bar of battery left. One bar and no blasted reception. Just as they crested a hill, she saw she finally had a signal and, with that, her phone began to vibrate in her hand as one message after the other poured in. By the time it settled down she saw she had six missed calls, an equal number of voice messages and more texts than she cared to count. Before she could do anything about them, though, her phone died—all the beeping and vibrating having drained the last of its charge.

"Argh!" she growled in frustration.

"Problem?" Nate asked, infuriatingly calm.

"My phone just died."

"No problem, I'll get you a new one. It'll be better that way—start over fresh."

"I like this one," she said doggedly. "It already has everything I need in it."

"It has what you needed for your old life—not for your new one. You've got a whole new list of people you'll be working with, communicating with. Besides, that was probably a company-subsidized phone—and you're not with that company anymore."

To her surprise, Nate took one hand off the steering wheel and reached across to take the phone from her hand.

"Needs updating, too," he said, giving the technology a cursory glance. "The one I get you will have better programming—and better access, too. I can't have you out of range whenever you're at the house."

"There's noth— Wait! What the hell are you doing?"

His driver's window rolled down smoothly and he lobbed the phone out onto the road where, to her horror, it was promptly run over by a truck coming in the opposite direction.

"How dare you? That was mine."

"I told you, I'll get you a new one. That one's no good anymore, anyway."

"No thanks to you."

She fought back the tears that suddenly came into

her eyes. This was a complete nightmare. Did he have to control everything? Maybe it would have been better to bite the bullet, after all, and suffer the consequences of her father seeing the DVD. Even as she thought it, Nicole pushed the thought from her mind. Her father's health had been declining in recent years. He'd ignored his diabetes for too long and the damage it had wrought on his system was beginning to tell on him, making him look much older than his sixty-six years. She didn't even want to imagine the impact a major shock to his system would have on his health.

No, she was in this for the long haul. No matter what it took, no matter the toll on her.

"The replacement had better be top of the line," she said, putting as much steel into her voice as she could.

"Of course. Nothing but the best for you, I promise."

"That's quite a promise. Do you really think you can meet it?"

Nate flicked a glance in her direction before returning his gaze to the traffic ahead.

"I'm a man of my word."

"That remains to be seen," she muttered, focusing her attention out the passenger window.

The way he'd said it, it held more threat than promise, and for some reason that, more than anything, chilled her to the bone.

Nate watched as Nicole was taken through to the fitting room of the third designer store they'd been to so far this morning. She'd insisted on getting a new wardrobe before eating, which now left him starving—but not for any food. He was hungry for her. For the feel of the texture of her skin beneath his touch, for the taste of her on his lips, for all the little sighs and moans she made while they explored one another's bodies with intimate precision.

Part of him wanted to say to hell with work—and clothes—and just head back to the house for another day in bed. Only two things stopped him.

The first was the office. Jackson Importers was his father's legacy in so many ways, and when Nate had taken up the mantle as CEO, he'd promised himself that he would invest every energy, every effort, into making the company the absolute best it could be. He didn't balk at long hours or working weekends, and even when he'd been stuck at home with a stomach bug, he'd still checked in through email all day long. Calling in sick on Friday had undoubtedly raised a few eyebrows. If he missed work on Monday, too, his staff would probably send an ambulance out to his house.

The second reason was Nicole, herself. Yes, he wanted her badly—both in bed and out of it. She was more than he'd ever dreamed of. He already knew she had a very smart mind—the dossier Raoul had prepared on the Wilson family had been thorough. If Nate could have found a way to headhunt Nicole Wilson for Jackson Importers after his father's death, he probably wouldn't have even needed to come home from Europe to take over the business. Her misplaced loyalty to her father was well documented, however, and he hadn't even bothered trying to steal her away.

That loyalty was the problem he was dealing with now. He supposed it had been too much to hope that her frustration with her family would lead her to welcome the chance to enact a little revenge along with him.

But her dedication to her father wouldn't be an obstacle forever, he rationalized. Sooner or later, she'd have to realize that Nate treated her better, and appreciated her more, than her father ever could. When she accepted that—and when she realized that the passion between them was impossible to ignore or deny—she'd turn her loyalty to him. She didn't know it yet, but he would be the best thing that had ever happened in her life. He just had to be patient until she came to terms with that—and watch her closely.

Yes, watch her *very* closely, because if the glares she kept giving him were any indication, any hand he reached out to touch her would come back to him bleeding. She was furious with him for forcing her into this position—and a smart, capable woman with a grudge was a dangerous creature, indeed.

So he'd have to be on his guard. Nothing new there—he was always on his guard. And he knew, far better than his father ever had, to be very careful before giving a Wilson his trust.

"Miss Wilson is finished now, Mr. Hunter," the store manager said, coming through with an armful of clothing and a smile that told of the sizeable commission she'd no doubt be earning today.

"So soon?"

"She has very specific tastes and was quick to decide on what she needed."

Nate gave the delivery address of his inner-city apartment for the clothing and handed over his platinum card, then looked back toward the changing rooms. Nicole was walking toward him in a new outfit, one that made his breath still in his lungs and all the blood in his body race to a very specific part of his anatomy. The ruby-red dress, while probably perfectly acceptable office wear on anyone else, skimmed every curve of her graceful figure. The scooped neckline offering a tantalizing hint of the swell of her full breasts. The three-quarter-length sleeves exposing her slender forearms. Forearms that led to delicate wrists and elegant hands. Hands that had gripped him and teased him and delivered all kinds of pleasure.

"All done now?" he asked as she drew alongside him.

"I just need some underwear and sleepwear."

"Sure. Do you want to eat first or keep shopping?"

"Still got that appetite?" she said, with a hint of an acerbic humor.

He looked her up and down very deliberately before meeting the unspoken challenge in her dark-eyed stare. "Always."

His reward came in the sudden flush of color that suffused her cheeks.

"We'd better get some food, then," she said sharply, breaking eye contact and giving her attention to the store manager—thanking the other woman for her assistance.

They stopped at a café in Vulcan Lane where he consumed Eggs Benedict while she played with a mixed berry muffin on her plate. While lingering over his coffee, Nate picked up the complimentary newspaper the café provided. He flicked through the pages, emitting a long slow whistle when he reached the society page.

"Looks like I might not have to make that call to your father's office, after all," he said, folding back the page and showing it to Nicole.

# Five

They danced together, right there in black and white. Caught in time forever. Their intense absorption in one another as clear as day on their faces. Opposite him, Nicole paled and drew in a sharp breath.

"Did you orchestrate this?" she demanded.

Nate laughed. "I'm flattered you think I have that much power but, no, I didn't."

She looked at him as if she didn't believe a word that came from his mouth.

"Obviously you want to hurt my dad, but why go to all this trouble with me over something that happened so long ago? Our fathers fell out. Their friendship broke up. It happens."

Nate looked at her over the rim of his coffee cup. Did she really think it was that simple?

"Your father accused mine of something he didn't do. He wouldn't listen to reason nor would he ever accept he was wrong. He broke my father's heart, broke the man inside him, destroyed his honor. And thanks to your father's actions, my father had to work himself to the bone just to make ends meet as he got Jackson Importers off the ground, ruining his health and making him die before his time. My father deserved better than that and so did my mother."

"And will hurting mine bring them back? Will it make it all better again?"

"No, but it will give me the utmost satisfaction when Charles Wilson is finally forced to admit he was wrong."

Nicole shook her head. "You're the one who is wrong, Nate. Let this go. Let *me* go."

Let her go? Before her father had learned his lesson? Before Nicole had accepted how good they could be together? Oh, no.

"Not going to happen." He picked up his cup and drained the last of his coffee. "If you're finished playing with your food, we should get the last of your shopping done before heading into the office."

They walked together up Queen Street toward Auckland's oldest department store. It amused Nate that Nicole maintained a clear foot of distance between them at all times. Not easy to do in the throng of business people, shoppers and tourists who congested the footpaths. When they reached the department store, Nicole lingered awhile at the cosmetics counters on the ground floor leaving Nate to hand his card over again as she purchased skin care, fragrance and cosmetics.

"You don't need to do this," she objected, her own credit card in her hand already.

"Humor me," he said, taking her card and examining it. "This in your name or under your father?"

"It's all mine, paid for by my very own wages. Is that okay?" She snatched it back from him and pushed it back into her wallet before gathering up her bags from the shop girl and heading toward women's wear upstairs.

"I'll get you another one."

"This one is perfectly fine."

No it wasn't, he thought. Anything that led back to Charles Wilson in any way was, in his book, tainted—and her previous earnings definitely led back to Charles Wilson. Nate had every intention of paying her a generous salary, and until that began, he intended to take care of things. Take care of *her*. Nothing but the best for her—he'd promised her that, and he'd meant it.

Upstairs in the lingerie department he was again relegated to a chair while Nicole browsed rack after frothy rack of underwear. When she'd finally made her selection and gone through to the changing rooms he got up from his chair and paced the floor. As he did so, his eye latched onto a stunning ensemble on a floor mannequin. The ivory lace-and-chiffon nightgown and matching peignoir was both innocence and pure sin in one simple package.

Attracting the eye of the sales clerk he gestured to the ensemble.

"Include one of these in Miss Wilson's size with her purchases, thank you. And, please, keep it as a surprise."

He flashed the woman a wink and a smile and the blushing clerk hastened to fulfill his request before Nicole returned from the changing rooms. Already he could imagine peeling the diaphanous garment from Nicole's lithe body, but not before he'd tormented both her, and himself, with touching her through its silken texture first.

It would be torment enough for him waiting for her to come back to his bed. But the waiting would pay off sooner or later. It would all pay off in the end.

It was well past lunchtime before they made it into Nate's offices in a high-rise overlooking Auckland's Waitemata Harbor. He settled his hand on the small of her back as they exited the elevator and directed her toward a set of glass doors emblazoned in gold leaf with "Jackson Importers" and its stylized logo of a bunch of grapes.

He reached forward and opened the door, holding it for Nicole as she walked through and into the reception area. His receptionist looked up and smiled. He introduced Nicole immediately.

"April, this is Miss Wilson, she'll be working with us from now on. I'd like you to call all the staff into the boardroom to meet her in about fifteen minutes."

"Surely that won't be necessary," Nicole protested. "I can just—"

"I want everyone to know who you are and why you're here," he said in a voice that brooked no argument. "Tomorrow I'll introduce you to the staff at our warehouse and distribution center."

She pressed her lips together, clearly biting back whatever it was that she wanted to say. He guided her down the corridor and pushed open the door that led into the boardroom. Seeing her there, in his offices, in that stunning dress, his self-control cracked. The instant the door closed behind him, he couldn't stop himself from sweeping her into his arms, drawing her against his body and lowering his head to capture her mouth. The second their lips touched he felt electrified, the charge of energy he got from her sizzling a slow burn all the way to the pit of his stomach.

"I needed that," he groaned against her lips when he'd sated his need, however temporarily.

"Well, I didn't. I'd appreciate it if you kept your hands, and all your other body parts, to yourself," Nicole answered, moving out of his reach and smoothing her dress in a gesture that spoke more of nervousness than any real desire to stay out of reach.

Well, he couldn't say he hadn't expected that. But still… "You can't deny you enjoyed it," Nate said, observing the brightness of her eyes, the rapid rise and fall of her chest.

"How I might respond to you physically is one thing. Whether I actually want to, is another. Don't touch me again."

"Ever?" he asked, narrowing his eyes.

"Ever," she adamantly replied.

"So you're telling me that if I did this," he touched a fingertip to the slight swell of her breasts visible above the neckline of her dress, "that you don't *want* more?"

Nicole fought to control the wave of need that trembled through her body. She couldn't show him any weakness, not for a minute. Men like Nate Jackson capitalized on weakness and she could not afford for him to get any more leverage on her than he already had.

"There's a name for what you're doing," she managed to finally say. "I believe it's called harassment."

To her surprise, Nate laughed. Genuine pleasure at her words making his eyes lighten and shine.

"You're priceless," he said through his good humor.

"Harassment. Would you have said it was harassment at about 3:00 a.m. this morning, when I—"

Nicole was saved from the torture of hearing him repeat what they'd been doing in the small hours of this morning, and saved, thank God, from giving him an answer when the door behind them opened.

"Ah, Raoul, please meet our newest addition to the team, Nicole Wilson. Nicole, this is Raoul Benoit. Don't be fooled by his name, he's just as much a Kiwi as you or I."

Raoul inclined his head in acknowledgement of Nate's introduction and gave Nicole a shy smile.

"Miss Wilson, it's a pleasure to meet you, and even more of a pleasure to have you on our team."

"I…" What on earth could she say? She couldn't exactly tell Raoul she was here under duress. That she'd virtually been kidnapped and forced to come here. "Thank you."

Raoul looked at Nate and she didn't miss the question in Raoul's eyes as he did so. The expression of supreme satisfaction on Nate's face told her everything she needed to know. Raoul Benoit knew exactly who she was and exactly what Nate was up to. It made her feel alienated, as if she was completely alone in this horrible situation.

Nate's voice broke into her thoughts. "I've asked April to get the staff in here to meet Nicole. I think it's a good idea to let everyone know she's going to be with us from now on."

His words made her feel like nothing more than a trophy, but before she could utter a word of protest, the door opened again. A steady stream of people came into the boardroom, sitting where they could and standing, lining the wall, when all the seats were taken. She was surprised Jackson Importers carried such a large staff in their Auckland offices, and Nate had spoken of a warehouse and distribution staff, as well. It rammed home the reality of what he'd coerced her into doing—working with the thriving and very competitive enemy. The next quarter hour passed in a blur.

By the time Nate showed Nicole to his office, her head was spinning and she was beginning to regret not having eaten that berry muffin at breakfast.

"And this is where you'll be working," he said as he closed the office door behind them.

Nicole looked around the sumptuously appointed office, at the amazing view of the harbor beyond and then back at him.

"This is your office. I can't work here."

He shrugged. "I'm prepared to share my space with you. All my space, Nicole. Together we're going to head up the most successful wine importation business in the country. Why would I want you anywhere else but at my side?"

That all sounded very impressive—but what did it really mean? "Is that a fancy way of saying that you want to keep an eye on me?"

He smirked. "I'll always enjoy having my eyes—or anything else—on you." Nicole huffed in frustration, and Nate continued, "If you're asking if I'll be watching your work, then the answer is yes. I know that right now, you don't want to be here and you're angry with me for forcing your hand. I think that'll change. I think that once you understand the opportunities for you here, you'll see that this is where you belong. When that day comes, you can have any office you want. Until then, you'll understand if I prefer to keep you where I can see you. After all, I'll certainly enjoy the view."

"What about privacy for phone calls and things like that?"

"Worried I might overhear your conversations?"

"Do you plan to follow me to the bathroom, as well?" she demanded, her temper finally fraying. Since his very unwelcome revelation this morning, he'd been controlling everything about her except for how she drew breath—and even that was under deliberation. Every time he brushed past her she got a tightness in her chest that was all his fault.

"Do you need me to?"

"I don't *need* you for anything," she said mutinously.

"Like your father doesn't need you?"

He knew exactly how to cut to precisely where it hurt. Nicole turned from him and tossed her handbag onto his desk.

"Well, if this is where I'm supposed to be, I'd better get to work, then, hadn't I?"

He smiled and gestured to the laptop and cell phone on the desk that he'd arranged to have delivered while waiting outside her dressing rooms. "They're all yours, have at it."

"Mine. Already?"

"I told you I'd take care of you, Nicole. I meant every word I said."

She swallowed against the lump that suddenly filled her throat. He said it like he meant it. As if she was something—no, some*one*—important to him. She didn't want to believe it. Couldn't believe it. They'd had a weekend of great sex. Okay, it was off the scale great sex. But that was all. There couldn't be anything more between them, especially not now he'd made his intentions toward her father explicitly clear.

"Where do you want me to start?" she asked, crossing behind the desk and opening the laptop, determined to keep this on a professional level even if it was likely to destroy her.

"How about you spend some time on coming to grips with our new internet-only business? It's taken off far quicker than we anticipated and reaches beyond our existing New Zealand market and allows us to trade overseas, as well. It cuts overheads considerably as, in many cases, we've been able to coordinate shipping direct between the vineyard and the buyer, thus cutting freight and storage costs to a minimum."

Nicole felt the thrill of excitement at learning a new business model ripple through her. For years, she'd been urging her father to consider an online ordering system rather than solely relying on hands-on distribution. True, hand selling often gave wine-store customers a chance to try something new that they might not have considered before, but to hope that would continue to buoy the market forever was professional suicide. The world changed at an incredibly fast pace. The wine distribution industry no less so.

Another thought occurred to her. Nate's approach to supervision had thrown a spanner in her initial plans to use her access to sabotage some of Jackson Importers' business, but there was still a chance to come out ahead here. Deep down she knew this situation couldn't last. Eventually she'd find a way to return to Wilson Wines, and Nate was giving her the perfect opportunity to learn as much as she could of their successful business practices and think about how Wilson Wines could implement them, or use them to create something even better.

Remaining focused on business was easier said than done as Nate pulled up a chair next to hers and brushed against her as he keyed in the URL that would take her computer onto the Jackson Importers portal.

"You'll need your own password. I'll get IT onto that immediately. While I go and sort that out, why don't you cruise around the website and make a list of questions you want to ask me?"

She merely nodded as he stood again, sucking in a deep breath of relief when he left the office. She'd thought her anger and resentment toward him would allow her to cope better with his close presence here in the office. The opposite couldn't have been more true. She'd found her eyes riveted on his long fingers as they'd flown over the keyboard of her new laptop, and had been forced to quell the memory of what those fingers had felt like as they'd flown over her body.

Nicole leaned back in the high-backed, leather office chair and swung around to face the view out over the Waitemata Harbour. Even on a workday the water was scattered with yachts making the most of the autumn sunshine and the strong breeze. How she wished she could emulate their freedom. But freedom was something that would remain in limited supply for her until she could work a way out of this mess. Somehow, someway, she'd find a way to get her own back on Nate Jackson, and, like his father before him, he'd be sorry he'd ever tangled with a Wilson.

# Six

Nate spent the rest of the afternoon with Nicole, discussing the wines they imported and the systems that Jackson Importers had in place both in New Zealand and overseas for distribution to their worldwide network of buyers. By the time the sun was dipping below the Waitakere Ranges in the distance, they were both looking pretty exhausted.

"I think it's best if we stay in town tonight, at my apartment," Nate said as he stood and stretched out the kinks he'd gathered in his back from sitting at his desk so long.

"Whatever you say," Nicole muttered.

"Would you rather head out to Karekare? We'll have to swing by the apartment and collect your new things first."

"I'd rather go home—to my home—but since that's

not going to happen, I don't really care one way or the other where I sleep tonight."

Her dark brown eyes met his in a silent challenge—as if she was daring him to contradict her. Nate knew full well when to pick his battles and she'd be disappointed if she thought he was going to rise to her bait this time around.

"Good then, it's settled. The apartment it is."

A flush rose in her cheeks. Annoyance, perhaps? Irritated or not, she gathered her bag and followed him out the office. She remained silent until they reached the undercover parking below the apartment complex.

"Is that my car?"

While she'd been interested and had plied him with questions about Jackson Importers all afternoon, this was the first sign of genuine animation he'd seen in her face since the weekend.

"Sure is. I have two spaces here. It makes sense for you to have your own wheels easily available, but we'll probably commute together most of the time."

She hastened out of the Maserati and he watched as she checked over her vehicle, examining every panel.

"It's a Roadster, right?" he asked.

"Yeah," she replied, finally satisfied the vehicle had come to no harm. "A '58 300 SL, to be precise. Good to see your people didn't do any damage."

"I only use the best," he replied.

Nicole eyed him over the soft top of her car. What would he do, she wondered, if she just jumped in, started it up and gunned it out of here? The instant the thought blossomed in her mind she knew she'd never carry it through. Not when he held such damning evidence over her and especially not now that the photo of the two of them last Thursday night had probably been brought to her father's attention.

"I'm pleased to hear it," she finally managed.

"Come on up to the apartment. You must be starving by now."

Now that he mentioned it, she was pretty hungry. She'd only had a nibble of the muffin at breakfast and had refused to stop and eat lunch.

"Sure, it's not like there's anything else to do," she said with a touch of defiance.

For some reason he gave her a look that she could only describe as approving. What? She'd subtly insulted him and he beamed back at her? The man was a conundrum, all right. A very powerful and sexy conundrum with an inordinate amount of control over her life right now. She may not like it, but she would just have to get used to it, she told herself. Even so, she didn't have to make him positively happy about the situation.

The trip in the elevator was smooth and swift and the doors opened to a corridor lined with expensive artwork. Her heels sank into the thick carpet as they walked to the end of the corridor where Nate swiped a key card and then pushed open one of two massive double doors and gestured her inside. Her breath caught in her throat as she took in the vista in front of her. She'd thought the view from his office was stunning, but this was something else. She could see over North Head and Mt. Victoria, out to Rangitoto Island and beyond.

"You certainly like your sea views," she said, dropping her bag on one of the wide and comfortable-looking leather sofas that faced out to the balcony.

"I do."

His answer was short and succinct and came from

right behind her. Suddenly she was aware of him. Painfully aware. Every nerve in her body attuned to the knowledge that right now very little space separated them. After that one kiss in the boardroom, he'd kept his distance. She hadn't realized up until now just how much she'd craved his touch. But she wouldn't give in. Couldn't. She had some pride left.

Before he could do anything, she stepped away, creating a void between them as she turned and faced him. A void that left her body silently screaming but which she refused to acknowledge, because that would only have her fall very firmly exactly where he so obviously wanted her, again. She might not be able to control much else in her world right now, but she could have some mastery over herself—however hard fought for.

"Where is my bedroom?" she asked.

"The master suite is right through there," he said, pointing down a wide hallway.

"No, not your bedroom," she said pointedly, "mine. I agreed to work for you. I never said anything about anything else."

"Anything else being?"

"You know exactly what I mean."

"Oh, you mean this?"

Nate traced the neckline of her dress with the knuckle of his forefinger, smiling approvingly when her skin reacted with a scatter of goose bumps. Nicole didn't move, she could barely breathe. One touch from him was about enough to send her up in flames. Already her entire body was invested in that tiny point of contact. She steeled herself for more, knowing she daren't so much as betray another measure of reaction.

"Are you going to force me, Nate?" she asked, her

voice deadly calm and at total odds with the swirl of desire that fought for dominance.

"Force you? No, I don't think so."

"Believe me, I don't want you."

"You don't want me—or you don't *want* to want me?"

She held her ground, refusing to answer, still not moving so much as a muscle. Eventually Nate let his hand drop.

"There's a guest bedroom and en suite second on the right. I'll move your things in there."

"Thank you."

Nicole allowed herself to breathe again. It was a small victory but an important one. She felt as if she'd conquered Everest.

It was Thursday evening, a week since they'd met, yet it felt as if it had been a lifetime. Nicole shut down her laptop and grabbed the overseas market reports she planned on using as her bedtime reading tonight. Sleep had been elusive these past few days. Knowing Nate was only meters down the hall from where she slept each night was unnerving. *It was your own choice,* she reminded herself sternly.

She'd been surprised to find Nate appeared unperturbed by her insistence on separate rooms, and it made her wonder whether she was alone in believing their lovemaking had been way outside the usual realm of experience. Maybe he was like that with all his women. She was surprised at the bitter taste that formed in the back of her mouth at the thought. How many other women lay in their bed each night reliving, caress by caress, the exquisite beauty of his touch against their skin, the possession of his body as it filled theirs?

She closed her eyes as a surge of need billowed through her body. It was just sex, for goodness' sake, she reminded herself as she shook her head slightly and opened her eyes. She could live without it. *Liar,* an insidious voice in the back of her mind whispered.

The office door swung open and the object of her thoughts filled the doorway. Her eyes roamed his body, taking in every aspect of his perfection from the hand-tooled leather of his Italian shoes to the sharp line of his tailored suit jacket. Slowly she raised her eyes to meet his, cursing the flush she knew colored her cheeks.

"I'm glad I caught you," Nate said, dispensing with any social pleasantries.

He was like that, she'd noticed. Charming as all get out when necessary, but straight to the point when it wasn't. Clearly she fell into the "not necessary to be charmed" pile now, Nicole thought with an internal grimace. *Or maybe,* that little inner voice whispered again, *he's just as frustrated as you are and this is how he shows it.*

"What's up?" Nicole answered, forcing a nonchalance into her voice she was far from feeling.

"Your brother and Anna Garrick headed down to the Marlborough region today."

"Judd and Anna? Why?"

"I was hoping you'd be in the position to answer that. We all know it's one of New Zealand's major wine producing areas but Wilson Wines has only ever sold imported product for distribution before."

"Oh, no!" Nicole lifted a hand to her mouth.

"You know why they're there?"

She shook her head. "I can't be certain. Dad pretty

much dismissed my study as being a waste of time and energy."

"Study?" Nate's expression became intent, every muscle in his body drawn tight.

"With the rising cost of international freight and the fluctuation of the New Zealand dollar, I thought it would be a good time to explore the internal distribution of a solid range of New Zealand wines. Wines not already being sold through major liquor retailers and supermarkets. The kinds of wines people might find in upmarket restaurants, bars and hotels. But make those wines a bit more accessible to the average consumer," she explained.

"Makes sense." Nate nodded. "Why did your father dismiss the study? Was it not feasible?"

Nicole laughed. "You think my father explained his decision to me? You don't know him as well as you think. No, he just told me we weren't pursuing it any further and not to waste any more of my time on it. So I didn't. Judd or Anna must have found my reports and somehow persuaded him the idea had merit."

"They've gone down to solicit new suppliers?"

"I'd say so."

Nicole fought to hide the hot rush of anger she felt toward her father for his about-face on her recommendations.

"You must have put a lot of work into this. It pisses you off, doesn't it, that your brother is getting to see through what you started?"

"That's a polite way of putting it," Nicole said. She was angry and hugely disappointed that she hadn't had the opportunity to see it all through. "I'd already approached several wineries whose management teams were very keen to come on board."

"Then I'd suggest you stop wasting time," Nate said, a half smile on his face.

"Time?" She felt like an idiot. What on earth was he talking about.

"Yeah, get down there and win back your business. Show me you can go at this with everything you've got."

Nicole looked at him in amazement. Carte blanche to progress her idea? Just like that? What if it failed? There were already so many wonderful and inexpensive New Zealand wines on the market, could it support more? Would there be a demand for the more exclusive vintages? And what about the upmarket imported wines they already sold? Would they be eating into their current business instead of growing new opportunities?

Her market analysis and research had borne out a definite niche of demand. Maybe she'd been too quick to let her father quash her idea. Maybe she just should have fought harder for what she believed in, what she knew to have great potential. Excitement began to bubble through her veins.

"Right, I'll get right on it," she said, reaching into her handbag for one of the backup memory sticks she always carried with her and powering her computer back up. She'd show Nate, all right. Success or fail, she'd show him, and maybe—just maybe—somewhere along the line she'd get to show her father her true worth to him, after all.

"Need any help?" Nate offered.

"No, I think I'll be okay. I'll start making calls first thing tomorrow and plan to head down on Sunday. I'd rather not bump into Judd and Anna while I'm down there so if I can work out who they're likely to be seeing first, and when, I can follow along behind and make an offer the wineries can't refuse."

"I like the way you think. I take it you have those reports on your drive?"

She nodded, automatically pulling up the files even as he spoke.

Inside, however, she alternated between disbelief that Nate believed in her ideas and the sheer joy of being told to implement them. She hesitated before sending the print command, waiting for him to reveal the catch or to shut her down, but, to her surprise, it didn't come.

"If you print me off a set we can go over them together. I'll order some dinner up for us while you do that."

Nicole nodded again, forcing her focus on the screen in front of her as Nate left the room. He was really going ahead with this. She'd reprinted her list of contacts and her feasibility study by the time Nate returned to the office.

"I've asked a few others to stay back in case you need them," he said as he grabbed a chair and pulled it next to her.

"Really?" she said, trying to control the sudden acceleration in her heart rate as his large body filled the space next to hers.

"We're a team here, Nicole. I wouldn't expect any of my staff to do this all alone. Besides, when it comes to you making an offer your clients can't refuse, I think it would be best if that offer came from a brainstorming session among us all so that it is completely unbeatable."

Nicole murmured her assent and concentrated on her computer screen as unexpected tears sprang to her eyes. A team. Even though she was here under duress, Nate still trusted her with all the resources of his company, backing her play and giving her room to develop her plan collaboratively, with all the help she needed. It was quite a change from Wilson Wines, where an idea of hers would have had to be fully formulated, presented and approved by her father before any backup was given.

It was a system that had probably worked well when the company first began, and it had been so crucial to have a clear chain of command to keep the business stable and the employees on track. But even when the company had grown past that stage, the management style had never changed. At Wilson Wines she'd had to fight for change tooth and nail, losing more often than not to her father's dictatorial management style. When she had her emotions in check she asked Nate a question.

"Has Jackson Importers always done everything by committee?"

She aimed to keep her tone light, teasing even, but she knew she'd come off as sounding critical when Nate shot her a dark glance.

"For the very important stuff, yes. When we succeed, and we do tend to do that a whole lot, we succeed together. When everyone has a hand in it, everyone works harder and feels far more satisfaction on an individual level. Why, don't you think that's important?"

"No, no, it's not that. I've just…not really come across that before."

"Well, you have only ever worked at Wilson Wines, right? Even on your school holidays? You never took any other kind of after-school job, did you?"

She was surprised he knew that information. He

seemed to know a terrible lot about her. Just how much? she wondered, feeling a little as if she was under a microscope—pinned, as she was, by his intent gaze.

"No, I didn't. All I ever wanted was to work with my father."

Nate's expression softened and, if she wasn't mistaken, his eyes gleamed now with something more akin to compassion.

"I know what you mean. From when I was very young and I knew that Dad was working all the hours that God sent so he could provide for me and my mother, I knew that I wanted to help him. I couldn't qualify soon enough. If he'd have let me, I'd have started with Jackson Importers straight from school, but he insisted that I complete university first, and that I take jobs and internships with other companies while I was a student, so I could be sure Jackson Importers was where I wanted to be. At the time, I was upset that he thought I didn't know what I wanted, but now I can appreciate the experience I gained. It helped me have more insight than I would've had if I'd only ever worked here."

"And then you went overseas?"

"Yeah, first of all for a bit of a holiday—again, at his insistence—then, while I was there I just saw so many opportunities for our company if they had a man on the ground right there in the heart of our major European suppliers."

"Your father just let you do that without any experience in the company? You must have been so young."

Nate shrugged. "What can I say? He liked my proposal and he felt we had nothing to lose by it. I worked my butt off on my own for the first few years and then, over time and as we continued to grow, we built up our staff."

Nicole fought back the pang of envy that struck her fair and square in the chest. What would it be like, she wondered, to be able to just pitch an idea and then have a free hand in following it through? Suddenly it occurred to her that that was exactly what Nate had done for her here and now. He'd heard her out, he was now examining her report and making notations on a pad of paper on the desk in front of him, and he'd assembled a team to support her in it.

Her mind reeled with confusion. He was forcing her to stay here—blackmailing her. Why, then, was he basically handing her the chance to see her idea through—an idea that her father had rejected—without any question?

There was a knock at the office door and it opened. Raoul stood there, his tie loosened at his throat and his shirtsleeves rolled up as if he meant business.

"Dinner has been delivered. We're setting up in the boardroom. You guys ready to join us?"

"We'll be through in a minute," Nate said. Once Raoul had gone, Nate stood and gathered up his notes and Nicole's papers. "Are you all set?"

"Sure," she said. "Just one thing."

"What's that?"

"Why are you doing this?"

"This?" he asked, holding her report up in one hand.

"Yeah. Why? It could just as easily fail and cost you a whole lot of money."

Nate shrugged, an eloquent movement of his broad shoulders beneath the fine wool of his suit. "I trust you, and I know you're onto a winner here. I can see it already in the work you've done to date. Why waste it? Besides, I can't wait to imagine the look on your father's face when we win."

"You think we will?"

"Don't doubt yourself or our team, Nicole. We're invincible when we put our minds to it." Nate crossed the room and held the door open. "Shall we?"

She nodded decisively and picked up her handbag and laptop and followed him through to the boardroom. Invincible. It should scare her that he was so supremely confident, but for some reason it gave her strength, instead. Strength and a belief that she could do this.

Hard on the heels of that thought she realized how much she was enjoying working with Nate. Too much, in fact. As an employer, he was the antithesis of Charles Wilson. She didn't have too much time to dwell on her thoughts, though, because once they entered the boardroom they were full-on. Nate invited her to explain her concept to the group in summarized format and then gave them his overview of her report. Over a selection of Chinese takeout they brainstormed ideas back and forth until Nicole barely recognized the idea as her own anymore. Even so, there was one thing she knew for certain. She was really excited about the direction this was taking and the fact that she'd been integral in instigating it.

By the time she and Nate went back to his apartment she was shattered, and yet incredibly buoyed up at the same time. They had a solid plan in place and she had all the ammunition she needed for when she went to win over any business that Judd and Anna might already have secured.

As she went to turn in for the night she paused in the hallway leading to the bedrooms.

"Nate?"

Nate was almost at his door and he stopped the instant she called to him. "Yeah?"

"Thank you for today."

He walked back up the hallway toward her. She couldn't read his expression in the dim lighting but as he drew nearer, she could see the half smile on his face.

"You're thanking me?" he asked.

She nodded. "For believing in me."

He shook his head slightly. "You're worth it, Nicole. I don't know why your father kept you under a bushel the way he did but, with your mind, the whole world should be at your feet. I'm just letting you use what is your own natural talent."

"I—I appreciate it," she answered, unused to receiving such direct praise. "I hate to admit this, but I really enjoyed this evening."

"Hey, there will be many more of those," Nate said.

"Well, like I said, thanks."

She hovered outside her door, her mind still humming with all the excitement of seeing her brainchild grow and expand into a working business plan. A plan she'd be implementing the moment her feet touched Marlborough soil.

It only seemed natural to brush her lips against Nate's cheeks and then, when that wasn't enough, to kiss him on the lips. He remained still for a moment but then his arms were around her and his mouth was hungry against hers. Her heart rate accelerated as she accepted the inevitable. They were going to make love. A part of her was glad of it, glad she no longer had to fight her instinctive and constant response to Nate's presence. But deep inside she knew she was, in part,

surrendering to him. Giving a piece of herself that
she'd held back. A piece she knew she'd be lucky to
get back whole, ever again.

# Seven

Nate backed Nicole against her bedroom door and relished the taste of her as they consumed one another with their kiss. He'd known it would only be a matter of time before Nicole capitulated to him again. With a passion as incendiary as theirs, it was bound to happen. Knowing that hadn't made the waiting any easier, but having that advantage over her—making her stay with him—had tempered his desire just enough to take the edge off. Just enough so that he could wait patiently and let her come to him as he'd planned. And now, at last, everything was falling into place.

It had been exhilarating seeing her in action today. There was nothing sexier than a woman with confidence and intelligence, and Nicole had both in spades. That she was perfectly assembled with features that could make even an angel weep was a welcome bonus, in his mind.

But now it was most definitely time to stop thinking and start doing. Doing and feeling. He reached behind Nicole and eased her bedroom door open, walking her slowly inside before closing the door behind them. Cocooning them in darkness only vaguely punctuated by the lights across the harbor that were visible through her bedroom window. He continued to guide her backward into the darkened room. At the edge of the bed he stopped, reaching for the zipper at the back of her dress and easing it down carefully before working the fabric away from her delectable body. For a split second he wished he'd taken the time to turn on a light, so he could feast his eyes upon her as he planned to feast with his mouth very shortly. But compulsion overcame his need to see what he was doing to her, to see her reaction to it. Instead, he would rely on his other senses.

His body craved urgency, but he held on to enough reason to know that he wanted to take his time, to stretch this out for as long as humanly possible. To give and to receive over and over again until neither of them could stand another second of the torment.

Nicole made a little humming sound in the back of her throat as he bent his head and traced a fine line from the edge of her jaw and down the cord of her neck with his tongue. Her hands gripped his shoulders as he moved lower, following the very top of the swell of her breasts inside the expensive lingerie he knew she wore. Lingerie he had paid for. Lingerie he'd tortured himself with all this week by picturing—wondering whether she was wearing the sapphire-blue ensemble, or the ruby red. Or maybe it was one of the other myriad feminine provocations he'd seen delicately wrapped in tissue before being placed in the store's shopping bag and handed over to her.

Here and now, in the darkness, he knew color didn't matter. All that mattered was sensation and, oh, God, she felt amazing in his arms, beneath his lips. He reached behind her, unsnapping the clasps of her bra.

He dispensed with the garment in an easy movement and reached with both his hands to cup the fullness of her breasts, testing their weight and lifting them slightly so he could bury his face in their softness before laving at the crease he'd created between them. He stroked the pads of his thumbs over her nipples, delighting in the straining peaks and the knowledge that his touch was making them harder, making her want him more.

Her hands let go their grip on his shoulders and moved to the collar of his shirt, unknotting his tie and sliding it free before her fingers were at his buttons, unsteady yet determined in their mission. He bit back a growl as her nails scraped across his chest, across his own sensitive nubs. Her hands shifted to the buckle of his belt and then, mercifully, eased down his zipper and pushed his trousers to pool at his feet. His erection strained at the restriction of his boxer briefs, strained for her silken touch, but instead, she scraped her nails softly along his length and he almost lost all control.

Nate eased her back onto the bed before bending to swiftly kick off his shoes and peel off his socks so he could step out of his trousers. He slid his briefs away, allowing his swollen flesh to spring free, and joined Nicole on the bed. Waves of heat rolled off her body, heat that intensified as his fingers roamed inside the fabric of her panties—sought, and found, the slick core of her. He played his fingers across her cleft, reveling in the heat and wetness of her body, knowing it was like this in readiness for him and him alone. She gasped when he brushed the tip of one finger across her clitoris, her gasp turning into a moan as he increased the pressure ever so slightly before easing it off again.

She pressed up into his hand, the movement making him smile. She'd been so controlled all week and now here she was. Her movements uninhibited. He gently slid her free of her underwear and then tugged it away from her body completely before settling himself between her legs. He felt her thighs tremble as he ran his palms across their silky smoothness. Tremble and then tighten as he lowered his mouth to her damp heat. He rolled his tongue across the bead of flesh hidden at her apex. Over and over until her body was so tense he knew she was seconds away from completion.

Completion he would give her. He closed his mouth around that special place and sucked hard, the action sending her over the edge.

Nate waited until the spasms that rocked her body eased off, then rose over her, reaching for the bedside cabinet where, as a good host, he knew there was a stock of condoms. He eased open the drawer and reached inside.

"They're not there," Nicole said from beneath him.

"They're not? Then—"

"I cut them up and threw them out. I didn't want to be tempted."

He'd have laughed if he wasn't so hard he was on the point of agony. Instead, he pressed a kiss to her lips.

"Don't move," he said, "I'll be straight back."

He covered the distance between their bedrooms in record time, then came back with a handful of condoms that he dumped into the still-open drawer, with the exception of the one that he ripped open and swiftly used to sheath himself.

"This time when you come," he continued, as he reached for the beside lamp and switched it on, "I want to see you."

She made a sound as if to protest but the noise cut off as he eased his length inside her. He gritted his teeth together, clenching his jaw tight as he fought to restrain the urge to take her hard and fast. To bring them both to a crashing climax within the shortest time possible. Instead, he moved slowly, painstakingly. She met his rhythm and he smiled down at her as she tried to hasten him in his movements.

"It'll be better this way," he said. "Trust me."

He knew it had been worth the wait as he felt her inner muscles begin to quiver and tighten around him. Nicole's eyes were glazed, her lips parted on a panting breath and her cheeks flushed. A fine dew of perspiration gathered at her temples. His own climax was only seconds away, and in the instant her body began to ripple around him he let go, letting her body wring his satisfaction from him. Giving himself over to the pulse that spent itself all the way from the soles of his feet.

Nicole lay beneath him, waiting for her heartbeat to return to normal, if such a thing were possible. It seemed that from the moment she'd laid eyes on Nate Jackson, she'd been in a constant state of hyperawareness. Colors were brighter, scents stronger and pleasure so much more intense than she'd ever known. She had no idea where this was all going to lead. She only knew, deep down inside, that she would probably never feel this much again with another man. The thought terrified her, because she knew this couldn't last.

She'd never been enough for anyone before. That's

why she hadn't been able to make her mother love her, or to make her father proud. And now she had Nate, who made her feel as if she could do anything...but she knew better than to rely on that. Because she wasn't enough for him, either—not on her own. He was only with her now to enact revenge on her father—once that was complete, she'd go back to being not enough.

Nate shifted above her, pulling from her body before rolling away. Despite the sternly chiding voice in her head telling her not to get too comfortable or too attached, she still made a sound of protest as his warmth left her—right before she froze at his next words.

"Let me get rid of this, we don't want another near miss like last weekend."

Every last vestige of afterglow fled her body as her blood ran cold. "What do you mean 'near miss?'"

"Didn't I mention it? We went to sleep like this that first night. The condom came off. But you're on the Pill, right?"

She wasn't. But that wasn't the issue. He should have told her straightaway so she could have gone to a pharmacy and gotten the morning-after pill. Being with Nate was bad enough but how on earth would she explain a baby to her father?

"Nicole? You *are* on the Pill, aren't you?"

"No, I'm not," she told him, a panicked flutter beginning in her chest. "Why didn't you tell me? What if—"

"I'll deal with it," he said firmly.

*He'd* deal with it? What about her? Didn't her thoughts or feelings on the matter count at all? And just how would he deal with it? Would he insist on a termination, or would he use a pregnancy as another tool to hurt her father? It occurred to Nicole that while

Nate had given her all the freedom in the world when it came to the workplace, he gave none in her personal space whatsoever. When Nate came back into the bed she had already rolled onto her side and was feigning sleep. She had a lot on her mind—and she knew she wouldn't be able to think if he was touching her.

By the time Wednesday morning rolled around Nicole had everything in the bag. Four out of the six wineries Judd and Anna had visited had jumped ship to Jackson Importers, due in part to the relationship she had already built with them during her feasibility study. And along with them she'd also picked up at least three additional contacts, who were excited about the prospect of widening their distribution.

Her days had been full-on. Judd had done a very good job of selling Wilson Wines to the contacts she'd had on her list, but she'd done a better one and it felt good to be on top. As she awaited her luggage at the baggage carousel at Auckland's domestic airport, she allowed herself a smile of satisfaction.

"Well, if you don't look like the cat that got the cream, hmm?"

Her pulse leaped in her veins as Nate's voice surrounded her in its velvet softness. She turned and faced him, willing her heart rate back under control. Willing her body to calm and cool down just a notch so he wouldn't know just how much she'd ached for him each night she'd been away.

"It went well," she said smoothly. "I didn't expect you to be here to pick me up. I could have taken a taxi."

"I wanted to see you," he said simply.

He bent and kissed her on the lips, a hard press of skin against skin and then he was gone again. She fought the urge to press her fingers to her lips, to hold him there for just a moment longer. Nate constantly surprised her. On the one hand he could be so over-bearing and yet, on the other...

"Oh, there's my bag," she cried, seeing the distinc-tive iridescent red case coming through on the carou-sel.

She'd been delighted with the set of luggage when Nate had had it delivered to the apartment before her departure, even if it was a little brighter than anything she'd owned before. Still, it was distinctive and cheer-ful.

Nate moved to collect her bag, appearing nonplussed about carrying such a feminine item as he placed one hand at the small of Nicole's back and guided her out to the parking building.

"Are we heading straight into the office?" she asked as he directed the car up George Bolt Memorial Drive and toward the motorway interchange.

"No."

"Oh, I thought—"

"I told them we wouldn't be in until after midday."

Nicole was surprised. She'd thought he would have wanted her to debrief the team and keep the ball roll-ing. Losing momentum with this could be disastrous, as Judd and Anna would shortly find out, to their cost.

Judd and Anna—that was a combination she'd never considered before. And yet the representatives from the wineries had told her that her brother and her best friend had worked quite well together, and had, more-over, seemed...close.

She sighed. There was a time when she would have been the first to know if there was a new man in Anna's life. The two of them had shared everything, and there had never been any secrets between them, until now. They'd been friends from childhood, her father's new housekeeper bringing an inbuilt playmate when she'd taken on the role.

They'd even attended the same private schools, with Charles picking up the tab for Anna's fees so his daughter would never be without her best friend. Thinking about it, she could see why Anna was so fiercely devoted to her father. Charles Wilson had given her the world on a platter. A world her mother couldn't have provided alone on a housekeeper's salary. If Anna hadn't done what Charles had asked of her, it would be like saying she didn't appreciate everything the old man had done for her over the years, and Nicole knew without a shadow of doubt that he would have held his own loyalty to Anna over her head in some subtle way.

She desperately wanted to reach out to Anna again. To mend the breach that had been caused by the conflict of loyalties. To rebuild their friendship if they still had that chance.

And while she longed to talk to Anna about Judd, and the rumors she had heard about the two of them, she also wished for a chance to talk to someone about her relationship with Nate. Nicole snuck a glance over at the man beside her and had to resist the urge to squirm in her seat. Just looking at him drove her crazy—she needed a good dose of Anna's gentle practicality to get her thoughts and feelings in order.

Nicole knew she *wanted* Nate—that was impossible to deny. Yet she still resented what he was doing to her, the leverage he held over her head. And underneath it all, she worried about what would happen next. How long would she spend as a pawn between her father and her lover, and how would it all end?

Nate was surprisingly quiet as they journeyed into the city and he handled the car with very deliberate movements, staying at the upper limit of the speed restrictions. By the time they pulled into the covered car parking at the apartment building she could feel tension rippling off him in waves. What on earth was wrong?

He stayed silent as they traveled in the elevator to his floor but the instant they were inside the apartment, she got her answer.

Nate pulled her into his arms and kissed her, really kissed her this time. Hot, wet and hungry. Her body bloomed with heat, moisture gathering at her center in rapid-fire time. Barely breaking contact with one another, they shed their clothing in a heap on the tiled entrance floor and Nate lifted her onto the marble-topped hall table. She gasped at the cold surface against her bare buttocks, but the marble didn't feel cold for long. She was on fire for him, resenting the time it took him to sheath himself with a condom. And then, thankfully, he was sliding inside her, stretching her with his hard length and driving her to the point of distraction as his hips began to pump.

Her orgasm took her completely by surprise. One moment she was accepting him into her body, the next she was flying on a trajectory that led to starbursts of pleasure radiating throughout her body. She clutched at Nate's shoulders, her heels digging into his buttocks as wave after wave consumed her, barely hearing his cry of satisfaction as his own climax slammed through his body.

It took several minutes for her to come back to reality, to realize just what they'd done and where. Nate rested his forehead against hers.

"I told you I wanted to see you."

Nicole laughed. "Well, you're definitely seeing all of me now. I was beginning to think something was wrong. You were so quiet in the car."

"I wanted to concentrate on getting here as quickly as possible. Believe me, the airport hotels were looking mighty good there at one stage."

He withdrew from her and caught her mouth with another deep kiss. This time with the sharp edge of passion assuaged, and with a tenderness she hadn't sensed in him before. It confused her, but then he was constantly doing that. In some respects he seemed to want to dictate every part of her life, yet in others he let her have her head. She could never predict how he'd react. She wanted to push back at him, verbally and physically sometimes, just to get a bit of space and control back in her life, and then he'd go and literally sweep her off her feet and do something like this. Something that transcended reason and gave her an insight into just how she affected him on a personal level. Or did it? Was she still reading him wrong—seeing what she wanted to see? There was no way to know for sure. She doubted she'd ever have him figured out completely.

Nate lifted her from the tabletop, allowing her body to glide against his as her feet found her footing. She shuddered anew at the skin-against-skin contact. There was nothing she wanted more right now than to prolong the physical link they had between them. In that, at least, they were in perfect harmony.

In their earlier eagerness they hadn't noticed the enameled brass vase had toppled off the surface of the table—its fall to the floor leaving a sizable chip in one of the tiles. Nicole bent to lift the vase back into its place.

"That's a shame," she said, gesturing to the floor. "Will you be able to get it repaired?"

"I won't bother. I like the reminder of how it got there," Nate said with a smile that sent tingles through her body all over again. "Come on, let's go take a shower."

It was well after midday by the time they made it into the office and Nicole was feeling the effects of making her 6:45 a.m. flight and the vigorous lovemaking she and Nate had indulged in before going into work. She made it through her debrief without making any mistakes or leaving any glaring holes in her rundown of who had come on board with them and why, and what she had negotiated in their individual contracts.

The meeting was just tying up when she overheard Raoul mention her father's name to Nate.

"...he wasn't looking all that good. Are you sure you want to keep this up?" Raoul said in a voice that was meant for Nate's ears only.

Nate flicked her a glance before turning his back to her and saying something to Raoul that saw the other man glance her way also before giving Nate a slight nod. Raoul gathered his papers and left the room, signaling the exodus for the rest of the staff. Nicole waited until everyone else had left the boardroom before fronting up to Nate.

"What's wrong with my father?" she demanded.

"Nothing more than the usual," Nate responded flatly.

"So what were you and Raoul talking about?"

"Look, he just mentioned he saw your father at a function over the weekend and that he looked more tired than usual. He hasn't been well, has he?"

Nicole shook her head. No, he hadn't been well. And her leaving Wilson Wines and working for Jackson Importers would be exacerbating that. Responsibility struck her fair and square in her chest as she realized the further ramifications of the business she'd just secured and what it would mean to her father on a personal level. She'd been so focused on beating Judd to the finish line, on winning the business away from *him,* that she'd lost sight of her father's stake in all this. Wilson Wines had been holding on to its market share by the skin of its teeth in recent years. She knew that better than anyone. And yet, with her usual impulsiveness, she'd just made matters worse for them. In particular, worse for her father's already weakened health.

"Nicole, it's not your fault he's not well." Nate's voice broke through her fugue of guilt.

She raised her eyes to meet his. "No, but my being here won't be doing him any good, either, will it? Did you know about his health problems all along? Was that a part of your plan, to take a sick man and make him sicker?"

"What, you think I want your father dead?"

"An eye for an eye, a life for a life. Isn't that what revenge is all about?"

"Nicole, you misjudge me if you think I'm capable of something like that. I'm angry at your father, yes, I'm very angry for what he did to mine. I'm furious that he's never admitted, ever, that he made a mistake in treating his best friend the way he did. But it's not his state of health that I want to change—it's his state of mind. Your father needs to stop thinking of himself as the one on top who is always right, and who can never be questioned. Don't tell me you haven't realized that about him, or that his autocratic ways haven't hurt you, too. *That's* the revenge I want—for him to realize that the world doesn't run on his terms. That he's made mistakes, and people have suffered as a result. Then he can finally start to take responsibility for the damage that he's done."

"Can't you leave it in the past?" Nicole pleaded. "Yes, he made mistakes, but he's paid for them, too. For twenty-five years, he didn't even know if Judd was truly his son!"

"You think that's enough to make up for what he did?" Nate sneered. "He *destroyed* my father. Do you know what that means? He sucked every last bit of joy out of him, every last bit of pride. With his accusations he tainted my father for life. Dad lost more than a friend and a business partner over your father's twisted blame. He lost the respect of his peers, as well, not to mention his income. The roll-on effect to my mother and myself was huge. Don't ever underestimate that. Life became very hard for us all. While you were still in that gothic monstrosity you call home, eating hot meals every night and wearing your designer labels, my mother and I were reduced to being reliant on food parcels and hand-me-downs."

Nate's words rained down on her like hail from a black cloud and, through it, all she could hear was the hurt in his voice. The pain of a boy whose father had changed and withdrawn from him. A boy who'd spent his whole life driven by the dispute between two men.

"But do you see what you're doing to him now?" she asked softly, all her earlier anger and defensiveness having fled. "You're the one in the position of power this time," she reminded him, "and how much damage are *you* doing by refusing to forgive?"

"Look, we're never going to see eye to eye on this and I'm not prepared to discuss it any further."

"Well, that's a lovely cop-out," she pushed back, not ready to let things go just yet. She deserved answers. "You think you were the only one affected? I lost my mother and my brother over the whole situation. Isn't it enough for you, now, that my brother is back? That my father knows that *he* is Judd's father and your father isn't?"

Nate shook his head. "It's not as simple as that."

"Yes, Nate. It is," Nicole insisted. "Judd's DNA testing proved he is Dad's natural-born son. The argument between our fathers was just that. Between *them*. Why let that keep affecting us now?"

"Because he's never apologized. Charles Wilson has never admitted he was wrong," he said stubbornly.

"And if he did, would that make it all go away? Would that change the fact that you and your mother suffered while your father found his financial feet again?"

"You don't understand."

"No, you're right," she said sadly. "I'll never understand. Too many people were hurt back then, Nate. Don't carry on the feud. It's just not worth it."

"I'm not letting you go back to him, Nicole."

"I don't think you can stop me."

"Aren't you forgetting something?"

"No, Nate, I'm not forgetting that you can still hold that DVD over me. I'd just hope that you'd be man enough not to."

# Eight

They went back to Karekare that night, their journey completed in silence, and once at the house Nicole said she was turning in early. She woke in the early hours of the morning to find the bed still empty beside her, a faint flicker of light coming from the main room down the hall. She got up from the bed and pulled on the peignoir that matched her ivory chiffon nightgown. The floor was cold against her bare feet, yet she made no sound as she padded along the polished wooden floor.

The room was in darkness, the only light coming from the massive LCD television screen mounted on the wall. Nate was sitting on the couch opposite the TV, a glass of red wine on the coffee table in front of him. Even though the sound was off on the television, he hadn't heard her enter the room, his attention fixed on the screen.

Nicole hazarded a look and instantly wished she'd

stayed in bed. There, in all their glory, were the two of them—making love. At the time she'd thought it would be a bit of fun. After all, she'd been the one to instigate it. Again, her rashness getting her into a situation she'd have done better to avoid. She closed her eyes for a moment, but behind her lids she could still see the images of their bodies entwined. Of the expression on her face as Nate did things to her she'd never allowed any other man to do. Of how she'd trusted him and loved every second of it, never for a moment thinking there could possibly be any consequences.

Opening her eyes, she turned and left the room before Nate could sense or hear her there. In the bedroom she yanked off her peignoir and threw herself back into the bed, closing her eyes tight once more— but not tight enough to stop the flow of tears that came from beneath them.

Nate sat alone in the dark, staring at the screen in front of him, at the evidence of the incredible connection he had with the flesh and blood, passionate woman sleeping in his bed down the hall.

He'd threatened her now twice with the DVD. The first time he'd meant it. The second? Well, he'd thought he'd meant it. Until now. Until he'd started to watch it again and had realized that he could never use this against her.

He still wanted his revenge against Charles Wilson. But he wouldn't—couldn't—hurt Nicole to achieve it. Her words today had struck deep inside him. Logically he knew she was right, but emotionally he was still that determined little boy who'd wanted to make his father's eyes smile again.

Nate had always understood his parents' relationship

was an anomaly amongst his friends' parents' bonds. Deborah Hunter and Thomas Jackson had never married. Never even lived together. Yet they were united as one on the upbringing of their son. He'd asked his mother once, when he was still small, why his daddy didn't live with them, and his mother had had such a sad expression in her eyes when she'd told him that Thomas simply wasn't like other daddies. Nate had never wanted to see that sorrow on his mother's face again, had never pushed for more answers.

It wasn't until he was older that he'd realized what it was that made his father different, and it was something that had made him even more determined to teach Charles Wilson a lesson. Thomas Jackson was gay. His sexual orientation had been misunderstood and even feared by others when he was a young man— if it had been public knowledge then he would have been touched by a stigma that might have seen him lose friends, not to mention business.

Nate himself was the result of a last-ditch attempt on his father's part to disprove the truth about himself. Thomas had explained it to Nate during his last visit to Europe before he'd died. How he'd met Deborah Hunter and, desperate to deny his own sexuality, had embarked upon an affair with her. It was a short-lived fling, but it had resulted in Nate's conception—a fact that had bound both Thomas and Deborah together as close friends for the rest of their lives. Nate didn't doubt that his mother had loved Thomas deeply, nor that he loved her in return. Just not in the way his mother needed.

The knowledge had explained a lot to Nate. Had answered so many questions he'd had but had never put into words. Nate knew his father could never have had the affair with Cynthia Masters-Wilson that Charles had accused Thomas of. It was something Charles Wilson should have known from the start—*would* have known, if he'd truly been a good friend to Thomas. But the man was known for his up-front, old-fashioned and often righteous attitude. In itself that was probably the reason why Thomas never confided his homosexuality to him. He had been afraid that he would lose Charles's friendship—and he had, even if it wasn't in the manner he'd anticipated. But Charles should have trusted Thomas, and the loss of that trust had decimated his father.

Yes, Nicole had been right when she'd said he couldn't change the past. But the little boy inside him still suffered. Charles Wilson had to pay. Nicole, on the other hand, had already paid more than enough, having to walk away from her home, her friends and her family.

Nate reached for the remote and snapped off the television. No, he wouldn't use the DVD against Nicole. The content of it was theirs, and theirs alone. But if he told her he had no intention of using it against her anymore, how could he ensure she would stay? Now that he had her, he didn't want to let her go.

Sure, knowing she was a pivotal member of the Wilson Wines hierarchy, he'd wanted to use her to hurt their business—and if her recent trip was any indication, he'd succeed quite well in that goal. And he'd relished the thought of staking his own claim on someone who Charles Wilson took for granted would always be there. But keeping Nicole with him was no longer just about pulling her away from her father. Now he just *wanted* her, for reasons that had nothing to do with anyone but him and her.

It was more than desire, he admitted, although that was in itself an itch he found he couldn't scratch hard enough, or often enough with her. No, he wanted Nicole in a way he didn't fully understand, and could never describe. A way that had nothing to do with his plans.

And the truth of that scared him.

She was still alone when she woke in the morning but through the bathroom door she could hear the shower running. She lay between the tangled sheets that were the evidence of her restless night and wondered what Nate had been thinking while he'd watched the DVD last night. Was he imagining her father's anger and disgust? Would he send it with a letter accompanying it, explaining that he, Nate, was Thomas Jackson's son? A son Thomas Jackson had raised while Charles had sent his own away in a fit of pride and anger?

The very thought of her father opening such a letter, or even beginning to watch the DVD, made her feel physically ill and she dashed from the bedroom to the guest facilities, heaving over the toilet bowl until her stomach ached with the effort. She flushed the toilet and leaned both hands against the basin, willing her body back under control. With a shaking hand she turned on the faucet, letting the cold water splash over her hands and wrists before rinsing out her mouth and vigorously scrubbing at her face.

She felt like death warmed over. In fact, when she thought about it, she hadn't felt physically fit in days. Was this all the toll of the days she'd spent in Nelson and Blenheim and the emotional demands of living and working with Nate every day, or was there something else she should be worried about? She didn't want to think about the night Nate had said his condom had come off inside her as they'd slept. She didn't want to believe that she could have been vulnerable to falling pregnant for even an instant.

Pregnant? Her stomach clenched on the very thought and she stared at herself in the mirror, noting the dark shadows under her eyes, the lankness of her hair, the pallor of her skin. It had to be the stress, it just had to be. She was worried about her father and under immense strain with Nate.

Nicole wondered again about Charles. It worried her to think that his health had worsened, and she wished she could get a fuller report. Short of visiting him, though, where she had no doubt she would be told in no uncertain terms of how unwelcome she was, she had only one other option. She had to ask Anna. Her friend would know the truth about Charles's health. She'd email Anna today when they got into the office, arrange to meet for lunch if the other woman was willing. And then maybe, just maybe, Nicole would begin to get her life back on track again.

Sharing an office with Nate hadn't bothered her before but today it most definitely did. She had to wait until almost lunchtime, when he headed out for a meeting, before she could compose the email she wanted to send to Anna. By now Wilson Wines would know that she'd wrested their new business from them. Would Anna even respond to her email? There was only one way to find out. She typed in the short missive and hit Send before she could change her mind.

She waited, drumming her fingers on the desk to see if Anna would respond. Maybe she was away from her desk, or maybe she was just ignoring the request to meet at Mission Bay for lunch. She couldn't stand it. She powered her computer down and grabbed her handbag. She'd wait at the restaurant. If Anna showed up, she showed up. If she didn't, well, then Nicole would just find out about her father some other way.

Nicole couldn't get over the relief that swamped her body as Anna made her way through the tables to where she was sitting at the back of the restaurant. Even so, the relief was tempered with a generous dose of apprehension as Anna sat in the chair opposite.

"I ordered for us already," Nicole said, hoping that Anna wouldn't mind she'd gone ahead and done so.

"Thank you, I think."

Dread clutched her heart. Was there to be no reconciliation between them, after all? If the look on Anna's face was anything to go by, twenty-odd years of friendship was about to go down the tubes.

"Oh, Anna, don't look at me like that, please."

"Like what?" her friend said, giving nothing away.

"Like you don't know whether I'm going to hit you or hug you."

Anna smiled, but it was a pale facsimile of her usual warmth. "Well, you weren't exactly happy with me the last time we talked to each other."

No, she hadn't been. She'd been feeling betrayed at the worst level possible, and she'd felt angry and trapped. A situation which she'd only made worse by yelling at her oldest friend, and running off. Nicole forced a smile to her lips and reached across the table to squeeze Anna's hand, the tension in her body easing just a little when the other woman didn't pull away. The waiter arrived at that moment with their Caesar salads and she let Anna's hand go. Once they were alone again, Anna asked her how she was doing. How she was really doing.

Nicole ached to tell her the truth, to tell her she'd gotten herself into an awful situation and that she couldn't see her way out of it, but she held it all inside, instead skating across the reality her life had become. But, she reminded herself, meeting with Anna today hadn't been about her. It was to find out how Charles was doing. She wasn't surprised when Anna told her he was less than impressed with her working for Nate. And, of course, Charles still had no idea that Nate was Thomas's son.

She asked about Charles's health, and was partially relieved when Anna told her he was okay. Anna wouldn't lie about something as important as that. What did hurt, though, was hearing about how easily Judd had picked up her side of things at Wilson Wines. She'd never been able to measure up to him, even though he'd grown up in another country. Always, she felt as if she'd been found lacking, and when Anna began to beg her to come back to Wilson Wines, to come home, she felt as if her heart would fracture into a million tiny pieces.

"I...I can't," she said, shaking her head, wishing the opposite was true.

"What do you mean, you can't? Of course you can. Your home is with us, your career was with us. Come back, please?"

If only it was that simple. Even if she told Anna about the blackmail, how could she admit the deeper truth—that she actually liked working for Jackson Importers? That she felt more valued and appreciated there than she had in her father's own company.

Nicole was ashamed of herself for even thinking it. She skirted around the issue and focused instead on the much-needed apology she had to deliver to the woman who had been her best friend for as long as she could remember. To her relief, Anna accepted the apology with her natural grace and they turned their discussion to anything and everything other than work, or men. How she felt about Nate was too raw and complicated for her to share with Anna just yet. She didn't even fully understand it herself, and until she did, talking about him was off limits. By the time their lunch was over, it almost felt as if everything was back to normal. As normal as it could be without them both returning to work in the same office.

"I'm so glad you emailed me," Anna said, standing and giving her an enveloping hug.

"I'm glad you're still talking to me. I don't deserve you, you know."

"Of course you do, and more," Anna replied. "I'll settle the bill, okay? Next time will be your turn."

"Are you sure?" Nicole had issued the invitation, lunch should have been on her.

"That there'll be a next time? Of course there will."

"Not that, silly." Nicole laughed, happy, on one level, that they were back to their usual banter.

But her joy was short-lived. Being with Anna had just reminded her of all she'd walked away from. All she'd thrown away with her reckless behavior. And now she had another problem to consider—that her impetuosity had possibly gotten her pregnant. That sense of fear and nausea she'd experienced this morning swirled around inside her again. Before Anna could notice she wasn't feeling well, or say another word that might see Nicole blurt out the whole ugly truth of what

she'd gotten herself into, she gave her friend a farewell
hug and left the restaurant.

The sunshine outside did little to dispel the cold-
ness that dwelled deep inside her. Seeing Anna was an
all-too-painful reminder of all Nicole was missing—
her father, despite his recent behavior to her, her best
friend. Even the opportunity to somehow carve a new
relationship with the brother she'd never had a chance
to know, and work with him to help stabilize and protect the family company. Instead, she was working
against them all—and enjoying it. Shame swamped
her. Somehow she had to make things right for what
she'd done. Anna hadn't mentioned how the Nelson and
Blenheim wineries business loss had been taken in the
office, but Nicole knew it must have hurt. She had to
find a way to make that up to them.

It was during the short drive back to the city that
Nicole's mind began to work overtime. There was most
definitely a way she could continue working with Nate
and yet remain loyal to her father and Wilson Wines.
It would be tricky, but hey, no one had made her sign
a confidentiality agreement. She could feed information to Anna on Nate's current development plans.
Not enough that it would immediately point a finger
at her when it came to light—and it most definitely
would come to light, she had no doubt about that at
all—but hopefully enough to give Wilson Wines an
edge against Jackson Importers. After all, in very
many cases they were competing for the same business, anyway. It would only be natural to assume they'd
continue to cross swords in the marketplace.

Satisfied she'd finally found a workable answer to
her situation, Nicole continued to the office, steadfastly
ignoring the conflicted sensation that what she was

about to do would hurt the very people who'd welcomed her into Jackson Imports with open arms. She swallowed against the lump that formed in her throat. If she could make this work, Charles would have to see her in a different light. Would have to value her worth to him. Wouldn't he?

Nate came from the 7:00 a.m. Monday morning meeting with his head of IT undecided about whether he was furious with Nicole or filled with admiration for her audacity. Over the weekend, while he'd thought she was sulking in her room, she'd been emailing information to Anna Garrick at Wilson Wines. Information he could well do without them knowing. At least, thanks to the tracking software he'd had installed on her laptop right from the beginning, his team had been able to find out exactly what information she'd passed on. Between the software and the team he had tracking her laptop activity, keeping an eye on Nicole had been an expensive investment, but well worth it if it made him aware that this was the tack she was taking.

But why was she doing it? She'd seemed satisfied with her success with the Marlborough district wineries. Then they'd had that blasted discussion, which had turned them back into silent ships that passed in the office, and in the night. Even at the Karekare house, she'd moved into another bedroom. He couldn't understand it. She was just as strongly attracted to him as he was to her. He knew it to his very bones. Knew it in every accidental touch from the ache it created deep within him and in the clouded look of suppressed need he saw in Nicole's eyes immediately afterward.

And it wasn't just physical. He was making every effort to satisfy all of her needs—including her need to feel valued and appreciated for her work. He was giving her every opportunity to excel at what she did best and yet it still wasn't enough. What more could he possibly give her? And why was everything he'd already given her not enough to make her happy? Was it truly that necessary to her to please her father, to the point where she'd throw away everything else he'd given her for the chance to make Charles Wilson proud?

He could cope with the collateral damage this time, but what she was doing had to stop. For his sake, for the company's sake, and for *her* sake, too. If there was one thing Nate knew, it was that Charles Wilson was a stubborn bastard who never forgave. Not his best friend, or his daughter. Nicole couldn't buy her way back into her daddy's heart with Jackson Importers secrets—she could only sabotage her own chances of succeeding with them. And he wasn't about to let her do that.

He pushed open the door to his office and felt a jolt of satisfaction when she jumped in response to his presence.

"I thought you were in a meeting," she said, swiftly covering her discomfiture.

Rain battered at the office window behind her as autumn's weather finally did an about-face and delivered on its usual wet and windy promise. The weather suited his mood.

"I was," he replied, his voice short as he chose his next words very carefully. "A very interesting meeting, in fact. It seems someone from our office has been feeding information about our latest initiatives to Wilson Wines. I don't suppose you'd know who that was, would you?"

To his satisfaction, she paled visibly under the on-slaught of his words.

"How...?"

"How I know isn't relevant. But it's going to stop right here and right now, Nicole."

"You can't stop me," she said defiantly, rising from her chair and lifting her chin. "If you're going to make me work here and I'm privy to certain information, you can't prevent me from sharing it. I haven't signed any confidentiality agreement."

"No? I would have thought that the DVD was enough of a substitute, wouldn't you?"

She wavered where she stood and he fought to control the urge to comfort her. To take her in his arms and assure her he would never dream of using the DVD against her anymore. But he had to stop her in her tracks. Had to keep her where she belonged, where she could be appreciated and valued—*with him*.

"Remember, Nicole. I can just as easily give you access to bad information as I can to good. Ask yourself this—how would you feel if what you were so merrily passing onto your friend at Wilson Wines was enough to turn very strongly to their *dis*advantage? What if it was the straw that broke their financial back?"

She sat back down in her seat, her face drawn into harsh lines of worry. "Have you?"

"Not this time, but don't be so sure I won't in the future. Now, let this be the first and last time you do this, or I will take punitive action, Nicole. Don't think I won't."

"I—"

She was interrupted in her response by the chirp of

her cell phone. He watched as she glanced at the screen and, if it were possible, paled even further.

"Your friend, I assume?" he sneered.

In response, Nicole snatched the phone up and dismissed the call, only to have it start ringing again a few seconds later.

"You'd better take it," Nate growled, "and while you're at it, tell Ms. Garrick that they can expect to have to do their own research and development in the future."

He turned and stalked out the office.

Nicole watched the door close behind him before answering the call. In the face of what she'd just been through with him she really didn't think her day could have gotten any worse, until she'd seen her home phone number come up on her screen. Try as she might, she couldn't fight back the feeling of dread that suffused her.

"Hello?"

"Nic, it's Anna. Charles collapsed this morning at breakfast. Judd's gone with him in the ambulance. You should meet us at Auckland City Hospital's emergency department as soon as you can. It doesn't look good."

"But you said he was doing okay," Nicole protested, at a complete loss for anything else to say.

"He has obviously been feeling worse than he let on. Look, I must get going. I'll see you at the hospital."

Anna severed the connection before Nicole could say another word. Shaking, Nicole grabbed her handbag and headed straight for the elevator bank. She slammed her hand against the call button several times waiting for the car to arrive at her floor.

Finally the elevator doors slid open and she dashed inside, punching the ground floor button as she did so.

The doors began to slide closed but suddenly an arm appeared between them, forcing them to bounce open again.

"Going somewhere?" Nate asked, entering the car and standing close beside her.

"It's my dad, he's collapsed. I need to see him. Please don't try and stop me."

Nate's expression changed rapidly. "How are you planning to get there?"

"I don't know, taxi, something!" A note of sheer panic pitched her voice high.

"I'll drive you."

"You don't n—"

"I said, I'll drive you. You're in no state to be left on your own." He reached forward and pressed the button for the level below ground.

"Thank you," she said shakily, watching as the car slid inexorably down to the basement parking floor.

She couldn't have said later on how long it took to get to Auckland City Hospital. The journey should only have taken about ten minutes but, as with everything since she'd received Anna's call, it seemed to take forever. The second Nate rolled his car to a halt outside the emergency department she shot out the door and headed inside, not even waiting to see if he followed her or not. Ahead of her she could see her brother and Anna. She strode across the floor, her high heels clicking on the polished surface.

"Where is he? I want to see him."

"He's with the doctors," Anna said quietly. "They're still assessing him."

"What happened?" Nicole demanded, turning to Judd, more than ready to lay blame for their father's current condition firmly at his feet. Life had been simple before he arrived. Not necessarily always happy but certainly less complicated.

"He collapsed at breakfast," Judd replied.

"I thought your being here was supposed to make him feel better, not worse," Nicole fired back before promptly bursting into tears.

God, what was it with her these days? So overemotional. She needed to hold it together, especially if she wanted them to let her in to see her father.

A nurse came toward them, "Mr. Wilson, you can see your father now."

Nicole didn't notice that Judd had reached for Anna until she heard her friend say, "No, take Nicole. She needs to be with him more than I do."

What was with that between the two of them? Were they a couple?

"Are you coming?" Judd asked with thinly veiled impatience.

Her tears dried instantly. How dare he act and speak to her as if she didn't belong. It wasn't her fault her father was in there, possibly fighting for his life. "Of course I'm coming. He's *my* father."

Nicole was horrified when she saw her father. Lines ran into his arms and monitors were beeping around him. He looked so ill, so frail. So very old. Guilt assailed her anew.

"What's she doing here?" he rasped, turning his head away from her.

But not before she saw the anger and rejection in his eyes. Nicole stiffened and halted in her tracks. The words of love and care that were on the tip of her tongue drying on her tongue like a bitter pill she'd been unable to swallow. She reached down deep and found what dignity she had left.

"I came to see if you were all right, but obviously you're just fine. You won't be needing me here."

She turned and pushed past Judd, desperate now to get out of the cubicle. Desperate to get anywhere where her father wasn't. He hated her. That much was all too clear. As far as he was concerned, she'd burned her bridges when she'd walked out on him and straight into Nate Hunter Jackson's arms. He'd never stopped to listen before, why should he start now? Well, two could play at that game, she decided, ignoring Anna who was still waiting outside, and kept her gaze fixed on the exit ahead of her.

Nate waited outside in the chilled morning air.

"How is he?" he asked, stepping forward as she came out through the main doors.

"He's about as much a bastard as he ever was. Take me home, please. I can't face going back to the office today."

Nate gave her a searching look before nodding. He wrapped one arm across her shoulders and gathered her to him.

"Sure, whatever you need."

The Maserati ate up the miles that led them back to the beach house and the instant they were inside she turned into his arms, wrenching away her clothing and then his, and pouring her energy into setting his soul on fire for her all over again.

She dragged him to the bedroom and pushed him onto the bed, sheathed him with a condom and then straddled his body. There was no finesse, no whispers of passion. Her movements were hard and fast and before he gave himself over to her frenetic love-making, he made her a silent promise. Charles Wilson would never hurt her again.

# Nine

Nate watched Nicole as she slept beside him. She'd been like a madwoman exorcising a demon. As if she was desperate to fill all the loss and pain inside her with something else. While he didn't regret that whatever had happened at the hospital had driven her back into his bed, he hated that she was hurting so much inside. Throughout the day she hadn't said a word about her father's condition or whatever it was that he'd said or done that had upset her so deeply. Even as they'd walked along the beach during a break in the bad weather, wrapped up tight against the bracing wind that streamed across the sand, she'd adroitly steered their conversation away from work and anything associated with her family.

Throughout their talks he'd begun to get a clearer picture of what her life had been like growing up. It hadn't all been a bed of roses, as he'd assumed. For a start she'd only had her father, and while he'd lavished his extensive resources upon her and given her every childhood heart's desire, including a live-in friend in the shape of Anna Garrick, he hadn't been able to atone for the fact that her mother had essentially abandoned her. Mostly, he hadn't tried.

After the collapse of his marriage and his family life, Charles had dedicated himself to his work. When he'd spent time with Nicole, it had mostly been in the role of stern authoritarian, making sure she did her homework, got good grades, behaved well in school. She'd worked hard to excel, hoping to win his approval, but his praise was sparse and hard to gain. And when she fell short of his expectations, well...

Little wonder that right now, Nicole felt as if she'd been cast adrift by both her parents. He knew she was in pain but he didn't know how to make it any better. He also knew that he was responsible for some of the scars she bore right now, and the knowledge carved at his chest with relentless precision.

He could make this all go away. He could destroy the DVD and release her. Even as he thought of it, everything within him protested. She murmured in her sleep as he gathered her against his chest. No, there was one thing these past few days had taught him and that was he never wanted to let her go. Ever.

Charles Wilson didn't deserve her. In contrast, Nate would do everything in his power to make sure Nicole wanted for nothing while she was under his roof. Surely someday, that would be enough.

Nicole poured her energy into two things for the rest of the week, work and Nate. By Friday evening she was shattered. Lack of sleep and the concentration her work demanded as she finalized every last contract for the Marlborough wineries had culminated in a thumping headache by the time she and Nate drove back to the apartment. She wished they were heading out to Karekare. The sounds of the waves and the birds in the bush that surrounded the house were just the kind of tranquility she craved right now. They would drive out there late Saturday evening, though, and she was looking forward to the time-out. Perhaps she'd even take Nate up on that earlier offer to learn to surf, she thought, as they waited for yet another change of lights before they could get closer to their final destination.

Her cell phone chirped in her bag and she ignored it. She should have turned the damn thing off before they'd left the office. After all, any calls she got tended only to relate to work—or Anna, who had been giving her unwanted updates on her father's medical condition.

Things were looking pretty bad for Charles Wilson but Nicole refused to let herself think about that. Refused, point-blank, to acknowledge that the one biggest influence on her entire life could soon be gone if things didn't improve. He hadn't wanted her there at the hospital. He'd made it abundantly, and painfully clear on Monday morning.

Was she so unlovable? Her chest tightened on the thought. Her mother abandoned her, her father now hated her. Even Nate only wanted her because of what it would do to her father and her brother. Nicole had never felt more adrift in her entire life. The pounding in her head sharpened and she must have made a sound of discomfort because Nate reached across to take one of her hands in his.

"Are you okay? You're looking really pale."

"Just this darn headache. I can't shake it."

He shot her a look of concern, his hand lifting from hers and touching her cheek and forehead before returning to the steering wheel.

"I don't think you have a fever, but do you think you should see a doctor? You haven't been looking well all week."

"Look, it's been a stressful week, you know that. I'll be fine. I just need a couple of painkillers and then about a month's worth of sleep."

"Well, I can't promise a month but I have no objection if you want to stay in bed all weekend."

She gave him a weak smile. No, she had no doubt he'd be happy to spend that whole time in bed with her, too. It was about the only time she could dismiss everything else and just concentrate on the moment, on how he could play her body like a finely tuned instrument. But right now, forget-the-rest-of-the-world sex was the last thing she felt like.

"Hey, I can change my plans for tonight. I don't feel so good about leaving you alone if you're not well."

"No, no," she protested. "Raoul's wedding rehearsal is important. You must go."

"If you're sure?"

"Of course I'm sure," she told him. Right now the only thing she craved was maybe a warm bath, those painkillers she'd mentioned a moment ago and then sleep.

In the apartment, Nate went straight through to the master bedroom to get ready for the wedding rehearsal and subsequent dinner that was being hosted in one of Auckland's premier hotels. Raoul had extended both a dinner and wedding invitation to Nicole, as well, but she'd refused, saying she'd feel like a gate-crasher. The wedding was tomorrow at midday, and she'd planned to go into the office in an effort to get ahead for next week.

Half an hour later she was on her own. She roamed through to the master bathroom and ran a deep bath, treating the water with lavender-and-rose-scented bath salts. Already she could feel the tension in her head begin to ease. She took a couple of headache tablets just before she undressed and lowered herself into the soothing water.

In the living room, she heard her phone begin to chirp again. She sighed, and gave herself a mental reminder to check the thing before turning it off. There was no need to rush to check it right away. If Nate needed her, and couldn't get through, he would ring the apartment, and who else would need to reach her right away? She closed her eyes and leaned her head back against the edge, letting the water and the pain relief weave their magic.

The water was cooling by the time she dragged herself out and dried her body before wrapping in a luxuriously thick bathrobe. There was no point in putting on a nightgown. Nate would only remove it the minute he got home, she thought with an anticipatory smile. Besides, her headache was completely gone now and she was ravenous. Maybe she'd watch a movie on cable while she had something to eat, she thought, abandoning her earlier idea of having an early night. And then, by the time Nate got home, maybe she could meet him at the door, dressed in nothing but a smile. The idea began to sound better and better.

First, though, she had to check her phone. Two missed calls, both from the same caller, and one voice mail. Nicole immediately identified her old home number and her blood ran cold. Had Charles's condition deteriorated again?

She punched the numbers to listen to the voice mail, and was surprised when the well-modulated tones of an unfamiliar woman's voice sounded through the speaker.

"This is Cynthia Masters-Wilson and I'm calling for Nicole Wilson. I'd like to meet with you for lunch tomorrow, one o'clock if you're free." She mentioned the name of an inner-city restaurant before continuing, "I think it's time we got to know one another, don't you?"

The call disconnected but Nicole still stood there, staring at her phone. Her mother? After all this time? She sank to the sofa as her legs weakened. Why now?

All her life she'd told herself she never wanted to meet the woman who had so callously abandoned her one-year-old daughter, never to look back, never to contact her or attempt to see her ever again. While she was growing up she'd told herself it didn't matter. She had her father, she had Anna and Anna's mother who was more Charles's companion than housekeeper in the massive gothic mansion Nicole had grown up in. Yes, it had always been easy to dismiss Cynthia Masters-Wilson as entirely unnecessary in her life.

But what did she have now? Nothing. Absolutely nothing. All week she'd been frantically trying to fill the emptiness inside her—working hard and playing twice as much so. If she was completely honest with herself, neither activity had managed to assuage the hollow feeling her father's rejection had left her with.

Reason told her to be cautious, though. This was the first ever, active contact her mother had made in twenty-five long years. As far as Nicole was aware, the woman had never spared her a second thought.

But what if she wanted to make amends? What if her reasons for leaving Nicole motherless for all those years were justified, her remorse for her absence in her daughter's life genuine? Surely she had to have a reason for finally getting in touch with Nicole after all this time.

Curiosity won out over caution as Nicole made up her mind. She would meet with Cynthia—she couldn't ever imagine calling her Mum, or Mother—and she would be seeking a few answers of her own.

Butterflies battled in her stomach as she entered the restaurant located in the historic Auckland Ferry building. She'd chosen to walk the short distance from the Viaduct, but with each step she'd come to dread her decision to attend. What on earth could they possibly have to talk about? And if her mother wanted to offer an olive branch, maybe even try to establish some form of mother-daughter relationship, why do it in such a public place? Surely a private meeting would be more appropriate for a mother and daughter reuniting for the first time in a quarter century.

"You must be Miss Wilson," said the immaculately attired maître d' as she hovered in the entrance, in two minds about turning around and walking back to the apartment. "Your mother is already seated. Please, follow me."

Too late now, she realized. The restaurant hummed with activity and most of the tables were occupied. The sun shined through the windows that looked out over the water, casting a solitary figure seated at a table there in silhouette.

Nicole swallowed back the lump that formed in her throat and focused on placing one foot in front of the other. She smiled at the maître d' as he held out her chair, not wanting to immediately make eye contact with the woman who had summoned her there. She kept her eyes downcast, fiddling with her bag before setting it on the floor beside her chair. Then, with a steadying breath, she raised her eyes.

It was as if she was looking at herself in another twenty-five years. Same eyes, same hairline, although Cynthia's hair now bore wings of gray, and while her features mirrored Nicole's own, there were lines around her mouth. Regret? Bitterness? Would she ever know the truth about that?

"Well, my dear, this is going to be interesting, isn't it?" Cynthia said with a tight smile.

Of all the things she'd imagined her mother first saying to her, that was most definitely not on the list. Nicole bristled.

"Why now?"

"What? No, hello Mother, pleased to finally meet you?" Cynthia gave another of those artificial smiles. "I don't blame you for being angry, my dear, but you have to realize that I'm as much a victim of your father as you and your brother."

A victim? Somehow Nicole thought that was stretching the truth. Her brother had already been proven to be Charles's natural-born son. Why would he have thought otherwise? Charles had believed his wife had an affair with Thomas Jackson. She couldn't imagine Nate's father having been the one to put that idea in her father's head, which only left one other person in that particular triangle.

"Ah, I see you don't believe me." Cynthia sighed. "I feared as much. Come, let's order, and hopefully we can talk."

Even though she didn't feel in the least like eating, Nicole placed her order with the waiter who'd materialized at Cynthia's request. Once they were each settled with a glass of wine, Cynthia began again.

"You're quite the beauty, aren't you? I'm so sorry that I didn't get to see you grow up. It was the hardest thing I've ever done in my life, walking away from you, leaving you with your father. But I knew he loved you, would protect you. Judd deserved the same, with me."

"How could you leave me like that?" Nicole blurted out the question. Goodness only knew she'd waited all her life for the answer.

To her surprise, Cynthia's eyes swam with tears. "Oh, my darling girl. Do you really think I wanted to leave you? Your father wouldn't let me near you. Once he'd come to his ridiculous conclusions about Thomas and me he wouldn't even let me *see* you. He had Judd and me out of the country before I could so much as blink."

She sounded genuine enough, and the grief on her mother's face certainly appeared real. Nicole found herself wanting to believe her, but an inner caution still held her back. Without being able to talk to her father, or her brother about this, she had no way of knowing if her mother was telling the truth. The waiter interrupted them with their lunch order and Nicole picked up her fork, playing with the mushrooms in her salad while her mother daintily tasted a sliver of scallop that had come with her dish.

"You could have written," Nicole said, still not willing to give an inch.

"I did. I wrote to you so many times over the years, but all the letters came back. I can only assume that your father had given the staff orders to return any mail addressed from me."

It was the sort of thing her father would have done, Nicole conceded, but there were still means around such a thing. After all, twenty-five years was a very long time. Nicole was an adult now—approachable in ways that were outside of her father's control. To never have been successful was a bit of a stretch of the imagination. Cynthia could obviously sense her skepticism and waved her hand in the air between them.

"That's all in the past now. We can't change that. But surely we can get to know one another now? Tell me about where you're living. Judd tells me you moved out a few weeks ago. I have to say I was very sorry to hear that you two haven't had a chance to get to know one another. I'm staying at the house now. I was hoping we could all be together again, the way it should be."

"Judd didn't tell you why I left?"

Cynthia gave her a sharp look before shaking her head and placing her fork down on her plate. She took a sip of the mineral water in her glass before speaking.

"He did mention something, but I'd prefer to hear it from you."

Nicole gave an inelegant snort. She'd just bet Judd would prefer their mother hear it from her. No doubt he'd already fed Cynthia a sanitized version of what had happened that night.

"My father and I had a disagreement about his plans for Judd. I felt it better that I be away from them both for a while."

"So where are you staying?"

"I'm living with Nate Hunter." She didn't want to let on about Nate's relationship to Thomas Jackson. As far as she was aware, no one at Wilson Wines knew him by his father's surname. Even at the office he was known as Mr. Hunter. "He's the current head of Jackson Importers. I'm working with him, too."

She watched her mother pale beneath her carefully applied makeup, her pallor making the lines around her mouth stand out even more.

"Would Jackson Importers be connected to Thomas Jackson at all?"

"It was his company before he passed away," Nicole confirmed cautiously.

Cynthia's brow furrowed for a moment. "Hunter? Would Nate's mother have been Deborah Hunter?"

Nicole stiffened. Had Cynthia made the connection? "That might have been his mother's name, yes."

"So, it was true. There were rumors that Thomas and Deborah were an item, but nothing was ever substantiated. Charles, of course, pooh-poohed the notion. He said if Thomas was having an affair he'd be the first to know about it." She made a sound that almost approximated a laugh. "As if he paid attention to anything but Wilson Wines. Anyway, I heard that she had a son out of wedlock, but since she didn't move in the same circles as I did when I lived here, I never really gave her another thought."

Nicole didn't know what to say. It hadn't been her secret to divulge and yet Cynthia had put two and two together so simply. If that was the case, why then had her father never reached the same conclusion?

Cynthia suddenly reached across the table, her slender fingers wrapping around Nicole's wrist and gripping tight.

"My dear, you have to get out of there. No one associated with Thomas Jackson can possibly be trusted. Who do you think lied to your father about me, ruining our marriage? Think of the damage that man's lies have done to our family. You have to realize, there's a lot of bitterness between those men. If you're with Thomas's son there can only be one good reason behind it—he's trying to get at your father."

Her words rang too true, as Nicole knew to her cost. Hearing it from her mother's lips only made her situation worse. She knew full well what had been on Nate's mind when he'd taken her back to his home that first night. She had no reason to believe his vendetta against her father had altered in any way. She was still his greatest weapon, even if through her own distress at her father's treatment of her she'd recently become a more willing one.

"Nicole, tell me, is Nate Hunter holding something over you? Is he forcing you to be with him?"

Her mother's astuteness shocked her and she bit back. "Is it too hard to believe that I might actually want to be with him for no reason other than that he treats me well and appreciates me?" Even as she said the words she was sure her mother would see them for the lie they were.

Cynthia shook her head gently, a look of pity on her face. "You love him, don't you?"

"No!" The single word of protest fell from Nicole's lips even as she questioned the truth of her rapid denial. Did she love him? How could she? She was his lover, his captive, his colleague. His tool for vengeance against her father. How she felt about him was far too complicated to examine in front of her mother. Instead, she settled for a middle ground, saying, "Our relationship—it's convenient for us both."

"Well, I certainly hope that's true, because I'm sure, if he's anything like his father, he has an agenda and that would probably be having some kind of revenge against Charles for when he kicked Thomas to the curb."

"Can we change the subject, please? I'd rather not talk about my relationship with Nate, if you don't mind. Besides, I thought you wanted to get to know me."

"You're so right. I'm sorry." Cynthia smiled, one that almost reached her eyes this time, and skillfully shifted their conversation onto other matters.

By the time Nicole walked back to the apartment she was in a quandary. When they hadn't been talking about Nate, or her father, Cynthia had been excellent company. She'd talked a great deal about her family home—The Masters, a vineyard and accommodation on the outskirts of Adelaide—and Nicole's cousins who lived there. Cousins! She had an extended family. One she'd never had the chance to know. And Judd had enjoyed the benefit of that, as well, on top of her father's total attention, her home and the job she'd loved. While she, even now, had absolutely nothing.

# Ten

Nate knew something was up the instant he let himself into the apartment. Nicole was nursing a frosty glass of white wine in one hand, her gaze fixed on the twinkling lights of the Viaduct Basin below, her body language shrieking a touch-me-not scream. Every part of her was tense, a far cry from the languorous woman he'd left in their bed this morning before heading out to Raoul's wedding.

He knew she saw his reflection in the massive window in front of her, yet she didn't so much as acknowledge his presence. A flare of concern lit deep inside him.

"What happened? Is it your father?" Surely he would have heard if Charles had passed away. That kind of information would still have filtered through to the guests from Jackson Importers who were at the wedding.

"No." she huffed a short sigh. "My mother, actually."

"Your mother? I thought she lived in Australia."

"Apparently not. Apparently she's moving back to my old family home. Seems like everyone has a place there—but me."

Despite her attempt at nonchalance, he could hear the pain in her voice.

"Did she contact you?"

"We did lunch together. Such a normal thing for a mother and daughter to do, don't you think? Except we're not a normal mother and daughter, are we?"

He was shocked when she turned to face him, her eyes awash with tears. Instinctively he reached for her, enveloping her in his arms and ruing the fact that he hadn't been here for her when she so clearly needed the support. His father had never said as much in words, but Nate had always suspected Cynthia of being behind the lies that had torn apart Thomas and Charles's friendship. Her poison had tainted the lives of so many people, and now she was here, poisoning Nicole, as well.

"You know," Nicole said, her voice muffled against his chest, "as soon as I was old enough to realize that I didn't have a mother, I wanted answers. Even after I convinced myself I didn't need her in my life. I still wanted to know why I didn't have unconditional love from her the same way all my friends had from their mothers. She wants us to get to know each other. Now. After twenty-five years. Can you believe that?"

Nate remained silent, knowing she wasn't looking for an answer. At least not from him.

"And underneath it all, I don't think I can believe it. I don't know that I can believe *her*. And in spite of that,

I still *want* to believe her, because what girl doesn't want to think that her mother loves her?"

Nate set her away from him a little, so he could see her face. "I don't think you should trust her motives, Nicole."

Nicole laughed. A sharp brittle sound that was nothing like the usual humor in her he'd come to know. "Funny. She said exactly the same thing about you."

He stiffened. "She did? Why?"

"Oh, she had you pegged from the start. Said you were probably just like your father. And she knew your mother apparently. Not well, of course." Nicole lowered her voice. "We didn't move in the same circles, you know," she said, in a parody of her mother's tone.

A chill went through him. "I mean it, Nicole. The way she's come here, after all this time and while your father is so ill—something's not right. She could have reached out to you any time in the past. I don't think you should have anything to do with her."

Nicole pulled free from his arms. "Well, that's my judgment call, isn't it?"

Nate knew he'd overstepped the mark with his last comment but he couldn't take it back now. He'd been speaking his mind and he knew he was right. Cynthia Masters-Wilson was not a woman to be trusted. And he didn't want to see Nicole hurt ever again. But he didn't want this to turn into a fight.

"Yes, it is," he finally agreed with Nicole. "Do you still want to head out to the beach?"

Nicole shrugged and took a long sip of her wine. "Whatever."

"I think we should go, it'll do us good to get out of the city."

"Sure," she agreed, but without any enthusiasm.

He watched as she finished her wine and took her glass through to the kitchen. She rinsed it and put it in the dishwasher and then went through to the bedroom they were sharing again. Her actions were wooden, automatic, as if she'd retreated somewhere in her mind. To a place he knew he couldn't reach. The knowledge chilled him to the bone.

Being at Raoul's wedding today had struck something home to him. It had been a happy, relaxed affair, full of people Nate liked and valued—and yet he'd spent the whole time counting down the minutes until he could leave, wanting to come home to Nicole. Being with her had long since stopped being about having his revenge on her father. What was past, was very definitely past. What he wanted now—Nicole—was very much in the present—and he wanted her to stay that way.

Nicole sat quietly in the car, mulling over her meeting with her mother. It certainly hadn't been the reunion she'd always imagined. Cynthia was a piece of work, all right. Coming back into her life after all this time and then thinking she could tell Nicole what to do. It seemed that all around her everyone was telling her what to do these days. And she was letting them. Everything in her life had become topsy-turvy. Even her period was late and she was never late.

Cold fingers of fear squeezed around her heart. Could she be pregnant? *Oh, please, no,* she thought fervently. *Please just let it be stress.* She wasn't ready for this on so many levels it wasn't even funny. She and Nate hardly had the kind of relationship that could sustain a nurturing environment for a child. Not to mention, she had no idea how to be a mother. She'd always been so professionally focused, so determined to excel in her work at Wilson Wines that she'd never given much thought to building a home and family. Even if she wanted such a thing, she didn't know if she could pull it off. And she couldn't bear the thought of proving her father's prophecy about becoming a mother and downsizing her responsibilities in the workplace.

Suddenly it was all the more important that she know, one way or another. With everything else in her life spiraling out of control, surely fate couldn't be so cruel as to throw her a curveball like that, as well?

"Could we stop at the shops in Titirangi on the way?" she asked. "There are a few things I forgot."

"Sure," Nate said.

When they got to the township he pulled in off the road.

"Do you want me to come with you?" he asked, shutting down the engine.

"Oh, no. I'll be fine. I won't be long," she said, getting out the car as hastily as she could. "Really, I'll only be a minute or two."

*Please don't come,* she chanted in the back of her mind. *Please don't come.* Thankfully, he stayed in the car and she walked briskly toward the bank of shops near where he'd parked. Where to go now? she wondered. If she went into the nearby pharmacy he'd probably see her and he'd no doubt ask her what she'd been in there for. He kept a full stock of over-the-counter medicinal products at both his homes so she couldn't say she'd needed any painkillers or anything like that. And if she said she was after sanitary products, and she didn't need them, that would just open up a whole new can of worms.

*Think!* she exhorted herself. The grocery store.

Sure, it was smallish, certainly not on the scale of a full supermarket, but surely they'd carry pregnancy tests, as well. She ducked inside the store and scanned the aisles, praying she'd find what she needed. Finally, there it was. She grabbed a test kit and made her way to the counter. On the way she also pulled some moisturizer and a lip balm off the shelf to add to her purchase. The kit, she'd ferret away in her bag. The other items would be camouflage in case Nate asked what she'd bought.

She was back at the car in under five minutes.

"Get everything you needed?" Nate asked her as she buckled her seatbelt.

"Yes, thanks. I'd just run out of a couple of things."

He gave her a studied look, one that made the hairs on the back of her neck prickle. She'd never been an effective liar. Never had to be. She felt as if the test kit in her bag was emitting some kind of beacon. As if any second now, Nate would be giving her the third degree.

"Right, we'll be on the way, then."

She sagged back into her seat with relief. She was overreacting. He had no reason to suspect her of anything, although he had to realize that she should perhaps have had a period by now. She counted back. It was just over three weeks since she'd met him. Only three weeks and they'd been through so very much. She felt as if she'd lived through a lifetime with him. Even so, it gave her a window of at least another week before he might start to ask questions. Questions to which she hoped to have the answer very soon.

The rest of the journey to the house seemed to take forever, even though it was only just over twenty minutes. Nate kept her attention occupied by talking about Raoul's wedding and the people who had been there, often drawing a quiet laugh from her as he mimicked some of Raoul's older and more eccentric family members. She detected a note in his voice, though, that she identified with.

Neither of them had grown up with a large family group supporting them. No uncles, aunts, curmudgeonly great-anythings. No cousins to play or fight with. Just a tight unit of parent and child.

"Some people are lucky, aren't they?" she said, as Nate's voice trailed off as they neared the driveway to the house.

"Lucky?"

"To have the richness of all those people in their family lives."

"I don't know whether Raoul thought it was particularly lucky when his great-uncle got up to make a toast to absent friends. Fifteen minutes he went on."

She laughed again. She should have gone to the wedding rather than have lunch with her mother. By the sounds of it she would have been in a much happier frame of mind right now if she had.

"Still, it would have been nice, growing up..." Her voice faded on the thought.

Nate's hand came across and grasped hers, squeezing tight. "Yeah, I know what you mean."

They were both silent as they went inside the house. Nicole made her way immediately to the bathroom, locking the door behind her and carefully removed the test kit from her bag. Her hand trembled just a little as she opened the box and withdrew the instructions. It seemed straightforward enough. She extracted the test stick and followed the instructions to the letter.

If she'd thought the trip in the car had taken forever, this felt as if she was aging threefold with every second. She counted silently in her head, refusing to look at the stick until she'd counted over the time the instructions said. She could hear Nate in the bedroom. She needed to get this over with before he decided to check on her.

Nicole forced herself to look at the stick. Stripe in one window...the other window clear. A negative result! A rush of exhilaration coursed through her. She shoved the test back into its packaging, and scrunched the whole thing up as small as she could make it before shoving it into the waste bin in the bathroom, and throwing some crumpled tissues on top of it. That would have to do until she could empty the waste bin into a trash bag later on.

She flushed the toilet and then washed her hands at the basin. Her hands were still shaking with the aftermath of the adrenaline surge she'd felt at the confirmation. She was relieved, immensely relieved, but hard on the heels of that sense of relief came a vastly contradictory spear of loss. Would it have been so very bad to have Nate's child? While they didn't have a normal relationship, maybe something good could have come from all of this. Something that could have healed the rift that had been driven between Thomas Jackson and her father all those years ago.

Babies brought with them their own very special brand of implicit trust and love. At least if she had a child, wouldn't she then have its unreserved love? A love that didn't come with tags and conditions. A love she could return wholeheartedly.

Nicole looked at herself in the mirror over the bathroom vanity and shook her head at her fanciful thoughts. She had worked damn hard to establish her career and she wasn't about to walk away from that now. Not even for some pipe dream of a perfect family life. A dream that would probably go horribly wrong if she ever tried it in reality, just like her long-anticipated meeting with her mother.

No, things were definitely better this way. She had no time or space in her life for a baby, not when everything was so horribly complicated—not now, maybe not ever.

Nate had begun to hate Sunday afternoons. In the past it had never been an issue. He loved his time here at the beach house, even more so since he'd been spending it with Nicole. But for some reason the coming week filled him with foreboding. Something was off with Nicole, too. She'd been different all weekend. He'd tried to put it down to her dealing with her feelings about the meeting she'd had with her mother, but he sensed there was far more to it than that.

Even when he'd reached for her in bed last night, he couldn't help feeling as if she was just going through the motions. He knew she'd climaxed, that wasn't the problem. No, what worried him was the mental distance she'd maintained from him. With the roller coaster they'd been through in these past few weeks, the only time the veils they'd held between them had fallen away was when they'd been intimate.

Now, they didn't even have that.

It worried him. Something had happened to change her and he had no idea what it was or how he could fix it. Talking to her elicited no more than a polite response and when he tried to probe deeper, she just shut him down by changing the subject. Short of holding her down and refusing to let her up until she admitted the truth about what bothered her, he had no idea of what to do next. What he did know was that he was losing her, and that was unacceptable.

He went through to the garage to double bag the trash sack to avoid any leakage, and put it in the trunk of his car. It was easier to transfer his waste to the massive trash bin at the apartment building in town than to leave it on the appointed day at the rubbish collection area here. Sometimes being remote from the city had its drawbacks but this was one he could live with.

Nate was picking up the bag and easing it into the second one when a tear suddenly appeared in the plastic and garbage spilled onto the garage floor. Cursing under his breath he scooped up the offending articles and pushed them back into the bag. As he did so, he noticed a small cardboard box that had been twisted up. The lettering on the box was not completely obscured, though, and he saw enough to pique his interest.

He separated it from the rest of the trash and unraveled the packaging. A pregnancy test? There was only one person here who could be responsible for this. He fished the used pregnancy test out of the package, but frustratingly, it was probably too long since it had been used to still show the result. But the fact that she'd taken a pregnancy test at all was enough to have his heart racing.

Every cell in his body demanded he march right up to her and insist she tell him the result of the test, but he forced himself to remain exactly where he was until he could recover some semblance of calm.

Nicole, pregnant? The very thought sent a wave of longing and warmth through his body. He couldn't think of anything he'd like better than watching her ripen with his child. Of sharing each special milestone along the way until they could hold their newborn son or daughter in their arms. Of having a family of his own, a family that included Nicole at its very center.

His heart pounded in his chest at the thought. A family, together, forever. It was everything he'd ever wanted and yet denied himself because he'd been unable to trust, unable to let anyone close enough to have the chance to hurt him since he'd been so twisted by the pain his father had undergone. And now he had the opportunity to put all that bitterness behind him. To forge forward with something new and right and special.

No wonder Nicole had been distant all weekend. She was probably worrying about how to break the news to him, about how he'd take it. He would have to take extra pains to reassure her he would take care of her and the baby, and that she had nothing to worry about, ever, while he had it in his power to take care of her.

Nate forced himself to put the pregnancy test box back in the trash bag and tied off the sack. A few minutes later, as he washed his hands, he thought about what he would say. There was no easy way to approach this. How did you tell the woman you had blackmailed into being with you that you wanted her to spend the rest of her life with you?

Back inside the house, he looked for Nicole. Through the windows he could see her out on the beach, her clothing buffeted by the wind. She was just standing there. Alone. Contemplating the life she carried within her, perhaps? How could he reassure her that everything was going to be okay? That she could trust him?

He reached a decision. He'd just come straight out and tell her. He'd learned a long time ago that occasionally you had to take risks—especially when something was as important as this.

Without taking another moment to think, he pushed open the massive sliding door and headed down the stairs that led to the beach. Nicole must have sensed him coming because she shifted her gaze from the seagulls wheeling on the air currents and turned to face him.

"Nicole, we need to talk."

"We do? What about?" she asked, her long hair whipping around her face in the stiff breeze.

Nate shoved his hands in his jeans pockets. "I know what's bothering you and I want you to know it'll all be okay. I'll take care of you. Once we're married, you won't have a single worry in the world, I promise."

"Married?"

"Of course. There's nothing stopping us. We know we're totally compatible. You can even keep working if you want to, I won't stand in your way. I know how important your career is to you."

To his surprise Nicole just laughed.

Nate frowned, somewhat less than pleased with her reaction. "What? What did I say?"

"Why on earth would I marry you?"

"Of course you'll marry me. We owe it to our baby to provide a united front. You, of all people, know as well as I do what it's like to grow up with two parents who aren't together. Our situation is not ideal, but we can make it work. I know we can. I swore an oath to myself that, no matter what, when I had children I'd be married to their mother, and that's what's going to happen now."

"What makes you think I'm pregnant?" Nicole asked him, taking a step back.

"You've been different these past couple of days and now I know why. I saw the box, Nicole. I know you've taken the test."

Nicole stared at him in horror. He'd found the test? What had he done? Trawled through the rubbish bins? Was he so determined to control every facet of her life? No, she pushed the idea aside. If she was being totally honest with herself, deep down she knew he wasn't like that.

"So, what? You think that if I'm pregnant that we must get married? That's being very old-fashioned of you, don't you think?"

She watched as his face changed, becoming harder, more determined.

"Old-fashioned or not, Nicole, my baby will not grow up illegitimate."

"Of course it won't," she flung back at him.

How dare he be so dictatorial? Didn't her thoughts or feelings factor into this equation at all? Just because he said something was a certain way, didn't mean it had to be so. Even if she was pregnant, marriage to a man who patently didn't love her would be the very last thing on her mind.

The fact that she was totally peripheral to his entire proposal was borne out by his assertion that his baby— *his,* not *theirs*—would not grow up illegitimate. Did he give her any consideration as an individual at all? There was no way she was marrying Nate Jackson. Absolutely no way.

"Good, then it's settled. We'll get married. It doesn't have to be anything big. I'm sure we can sort something out within the next few weeks."

"You can't treat me like some possession to be ordered about. I'm a human being. I've already had quite enough of that kind of treatment from my own father and I certainly won't put up with it from you." She drew up short as a new thought had occurred to her. "My father...is that what this is about? Do you want to get married to rub it in his face? Is this the next part of your revenge?"

"No!" His protest was immediate, and almost seemed instinctive, but how could she believe him? He'd been following his plan of payback right from the start. How was she to know this wasn't his next step?

"Really?" she drawled.

"Look, I know this wasn't the most romantic of proposals—"

"Romantic?" She laughed again, a harsh sound that came from a place deep inside her. A place that hurt with an ache that throbbed through her entire body. "Sort out what you like, Nate, but I'm not marrying you. There were two possible outcomes when I took that test. One, that I was pregnant, the other, that I wasn't. I'm not pregnant, and I'm not marrying you, so you can shove your proposal right back where it came from."

She pushed past him and strode on up the beach toward the house. She thought he couldn't hurt her any more than he already had done. She'd thought that perhaps they'd found a workable solution to their situation. She did enjoy her work at Jackson Importers. She had a freedom there that she didn't have at Wilson Wines and she loved the opportunity to spread her wings and to brainstorm her ideas with others who were on the same wavelength. And she couldn't argue that she and Nate were exquisitely compatible in the bedroom. It had been about the only thing that had kept her sane these past weeks. Knowing that she could seek, and find, oblivion in his arms at night.

But right now she was so angry she could barely see the steps in front of her. She went inside the house, sliding the glass door closed so hard the panes inside it wobbled. Through the window she saw Nate standing on the beach, his hands still in his pockets as he faced the house.

Childishly, she wanted nothing more right now than to flip him the bird, but she wouldn't lower herself to that level. Instead, she turned away from the glass and tried to bring her roiling emotions under control.

Damn him. Damn him for asking her to marry him that way. For asking her to marry him at all! She didn't want to marry, she just wanted to be able to do her job. A job was something she could measure herself by. It had no feelings and only relied on her showing up every single day and giving her very best. A job wouldn't hurt her when the going got rough.

And yet, she couldn't help wondering how she would have felt if the situation had been different. If she had been pregnant, after all—if Nate's proposal had come from a different angle where he'd expressed a desire to have a family with her, even expressed affection or maybe even love for her—would she have been so quick to turn down Nate's suggestion? Nicole knew in her heart her response would have been "yes." She felt the same way he did about raising a child in a unified relationship. In a stable and loving environment. It had been a dream of hers from when she was a little girl. She and Anna had played families, both of them pretending their respective man-about-the-house was at work while they cared for their doll-babies with infinite maternal care.

No, she had to be honest with herself. No matter her feelings for Nate—feelings she couldn't quite put into words—with no mention of love spoken between them, they would only have been setting themselves up for failure. It took a committed parent to raise a child and parents who were not committed to one another, and yet still lived under the same roof, only created a divisive and, in the long term, unhappy home.

And that, sadly, left her right back where she'd started. A pawn in a game where she held none of the moveable pieces. Waiting for the inevitable checkmate when Nate reached his goal against Wilson Wines.

She wanted out of this horrible situation. She wanted out, right now. But how?

# Eleven

Nate lay in the bed listening to Nicole breathe, her back as firmly presented to him as it had been when they went to bed. She had barely spoken more than a handful of words to him since the beach and he could hardly blame her. He'd been careless and stupid—thinking only of himself and what he wanted.

He'd used her shamelessly for weeks and expected her to simply roll over and agree to his demand without a single consideration for what it meant to her.

One thing he'd learned from this was that his feelings for her went far deeper than those of revenge. Far deeper than he'd ever wanted to acknowledge. Understanding had struck when she'd accused him of proposing as part of his revenge. That's when he'd realized that her father hadn't even crossed his mind when he'd found the pregnancy test. All he'd thought of was Nicole, and the child they might be having together.

He knew, now, that everything that mattered in his life was tied to the woman who lay in the darkness beside him—beside him yet not touching him and not allowing him to touch her. The woman who'd rejected him most emphatically on the sandy shore outside.

Nate wasn't the type of person who took no for an answer, yet in this he had to. He had no other choice. He'd messed things up between them, well and truly, and he could see no clear way to fix them.

He still had her here in his life, would continue to do so while he could hold the DVD over her. But what did that prove? Nothing. It only proved that, given the choice, she wouldn't be with him and that truth was the most painful of all.

He knew now that he loved her. He didn't want to imagine a life without her. These past weeks had been an eye opener for him. From the start he'd been attracted to her, but that attraction had very rapidly gone far deeper than merely a face-to-face—or skin-to-skin—appreciation of one another. He hadn't wanted to admit it to himself but her rejection had forced him to be honest.

Nate didn't just want to marry her to provide for her and their unborn child—the child that had existed only in his imagination. He wanted the whole shebang. He wanted to love Nicole and spend the rest of his life loving her. And being loved by her in return. He wanted to marry her, for *her*.

Problem solving had always come naturally to him. It was one of the things that made him good at his job—being able to see solutions before anyone else even fully understood the problem. Yet in this he was helpless.

How on earth could he convince her that his intentions toward her came from his heart? He'd tried to lay it on the line on the beach, but he'd gone about it in entirely the wrong way. Had told her, rather than asking her, how things were going to be. With each syllable he'd destroyed every last chance of creating the reality he had really wanted all along.

This was his mess. And for the first time in his life he didn't have a plan for dealing with it.

He pushed back the bedcovers and rose, leaving the room on a silent tread. Streaks of moonlight lit the rest of the house, cold and gray, just like the future that stretched ahead of him without Nicole willingly by his side. It was no better than he deserved for the way he'd treated her, but he didn't want to accept that. Couldn't accept that this was all over. Somehow he would find a solution. It was what he did. And this time, his very happiness depended on it.

They'd remained civil to one another, at least that was something she could be grateful for, Nicole thought as she studied the distribution reports that had been sent for her perusal. Civility was one thing, but how on earth would they continue to live together? Already she could feel the strain between them. She'd had no appetite for anything all day and she knew that food would not ease the hollow that echoed inside her.

Nate had told her to bring her own car into work today as he would be working late entertaining overseas clients. She hadn't suggested she assist him as she was only too grateful for the excuse to put a little distance between them. Leaving the office was a relief.

At the apartment, she'd barely had time to put her laptop case down when the phone began to ring. She let the answering machine pick up but hastened to lift the receiver when her mother's voice could be heard through the speaker.

"Hello?"

"Nicole, darling, I was hoping to catch you at home. How was the rest of your weekend?"

"It was fine. We went out to the beach house."

"I see. Have you thought any more about what I said to you about the Jacksons? I really don't think it's a good idea for you to spend any more time under that man's roof. Seriously, my dear, nothing good will come of it. Surely you can see that."

Another person telling her what to do. Nicole fought back the sigh that built in her chest.

"I'm an adult, Cynthia, and I'm long used to making my own decisions."

"I know, but allow me a mother's care in this instance. I know I wasn't there for you growing up, but trust me when I say I do know better in this case."

"Was there anything else you rang me for?" Nicole asked, struggling with a desire to hang up before she was bossed around again.

"Yes, well, there is, actually."

Was it Nicole's imagination or did her mother sound a little upset? She waited, saying nothing, until Cynthia continued.

"Things haven't really worked out here the way I'd thought they would and I've decided to go back to Adelaide for now. I'd really love it if you could come with me. I'm leaving in the morning and I'll leave a ticket for you at the check-in desk."

"I really don't think—" Nicole started, only to be shut down by Cynthia's voice talking over her.

"No, please, don't make a decision right this minute. Take the evening to think it over. We really haven't had a chance to get to know one another, have we? After all, one lunch together does not a relationship make." She laughed at that, the sound ringing false to Nicole's ears. "At The Masters' we could just spend some time learning to understand one another a little better and you would have the chance to meet up with some of your cousins—get to know your extended family. After all, you're a Masters by blood, and you have every right to be there with me. It's your heritage, too."

Nicole felt a throbbing pain start behind one eye. Did Cynthia instinctively know all of Nicole's hot buttons? But to leave, now, just like that? With her father still direly ill in the hospital and with Nate still holding the DVD over her head?

"Okay, I'll think about it," she conceded.

"You will? Oh, that's marvelous." She gave Nicole the flight time and details. "I'll expect to see you in the departure lounge, then. I can't wait."

Cynthia hung up before Nicole could say another word and Nicole replaced the handset of the phone on its station, a sensation of numbness enveloping her body.

Her life was in tatters. Could her mother's offer be the new beginning she really, desperately, needed? Could she just walk away and say to hell with the consequences of what would happen when Nate gave her father the DVD? She had no doubt he would do it. If she'd learned anything about Nate in this time, it was just how far he was prepared to go to get what he wanted. He wouldn't rest until he'd pulled her family down from its pedestal. She'd already done her part—he didn't need her anymore. When you got right down to it, she was as disposable to him as she was to her father.

Was she prepared to let him hurt her father like that without even trying to interfere? Was she ready to end their affair, once and for all? Could she really, in all honesty, walk away?

Nate woke to an empty bed. Nicole had been sound asleep when he'd come in last night, a little the worse for wear after a few drinks with his hard-drinking clients. His head gave him a solid reminder that drinking on an empty stomach was not conducive to clear brain function the next day. He felt across the bed. Her side was stone cold. A glance at the bedside clock confirmed it was much later than they usually rose. Obviously she'd left him to it and gone into the office already.

He dragged himself from the bed and through to the kitchen where he downed the better part of the liter of orange juice that was in the fridge, then grabbed a banana from the fruit bowl. It was all he had time for. He'd have to make up for it later in the day.

Showering and dressing took more effort than he wanted to admit and, concerned he may still be over the safe driving limit, he caught a taxi to the office. Nicole had her car there so they could travel home together at the end of the day.

"Is Miss Wilson not with you this morning?" April asked as he entered the office.

Nate felt the first pang of warning. "Isn't she already in the office?"

"No, she left a note for me saying she wouldn't be in. I thought she would be arriving with you."

Nate felt his blood run cold in his veins. She'd been into the office already?

"Let me know if she calls, will you?" he directed as

he strode through to his office and rang the concierge of the apartment building.

Five minutes later he had confirmation that her car had left the parking garage a little after five this morning. Another call confirmed she'd swiped in at the office block parking floor shortly after, but that she'd left again within ten minutes. Which begged the question. Where the hell was she now?

He punched the redial on his office phone for the seventh time this morning, only to get the same automated message—that her phone was either switched off or outside of the calling area. He thought about his own cell phone, which had been damnably silent all morning, and reached into his pocket.

Sometime during the night he'd turned it off while he was out and hadn't turned it back on again. He must have been more intoxicated than he'd realized. Nate thumbed the on button and waited for the phone to power up. The instant it had connected to its service provider the screen flashed up—one missed call, one message. Cursing himself for all kinds of idiocy, he hit the numbers required to play the message. Nicole's shaking voice filled his ears.

"I can't stay with you anymore, Nate. It's slowly killing me inside. Do what you like with the DVD. I don't care anymore. I just know that if I don't get some distance, from you, from everyone, I'm going to go insane. All my life I've tried to be everything for everyone. I even had to do it with you, but I can't do it anymore, not now, not ever again. It's all too much. I need to take care of *me* and to learn to put myself first for a change. In fact, I need to find out who I really am, and what I want. I'm sick to death of being told.

My mother has asked me to go with her to Adelaide. Please don't bother trying to contact me again."

She'd left the message at about six o'clock this morning and it sounded as if she was crying toward the end, as if she was teetering on the edge of a breakdown. Nate felt every muscle in his body clench as the urge to protect her fired through him. He had to find her, needed to find her. As vulnerable as she was right now, she needed a champion. Someone to watch over her while she got her act back together. Someone like him. Certainly not someone like Cynthia Masters-Wilson.

Nate remembered the GPS device in her phone, the one that could track where she was at any given time. He called through to his IT guy, Max, who promised to get on it and let him know within the next few minutes where her phone was. In the meantime, Nate hit the search function on his desktop computer and keyed in Auckland International Airport's departures. Hopefully he wouldn't be too late to stop her from leaving on the flight for Adelaide.

Hope died a swift and sudden death when he saw the only direct flight to Adelaide that morning had departed at eight o'clock. The time she left the apartment, the time she'd left the message for him—it all fit with her being on that flight out of the country. The flight with her mother.

Anger and frustration vied for dominance as he weighed up the idea of booking the next available plane to Australia and making his way to Adelaide to get Nicole back. He wouldn't put it past Nicole to refuse to see him, though, nor her mother to prevent him from making any contact with her. Even if he could track her now it wouldn't be much use to him.

His phone rang on his desk and he swept the receiver up.

"Nate, the tracker shows this address for the phone. Are you sure she's not hiding in your office somewhere?"

Nate bit back the growl of frustration at his computer geek's humor. He reached across and opened a drawer where Nicole had often put her things during the day. There, in all its totally specced-up splendor, lay her cell phone. A sticky note on the screen said, *I won't be needing this anymore,* in Nicole's handwriting. Nate slowly slid the drawer closed and thanked Max for the information, then hung up the phone and, propping his elbows on the desk, rested his head in his hands.

The headache he'd woken with was nothing compared to how he felt now. He closed his eyes for a moment and thought hard about what he should do next. Flying to Adelaide was a definite option, but before he did that he needed some ammunition behind him and what better ammunition than her brother's support?

Nate went to grab his keys, then cursed anew as he remembered he'd left his car at the apartment. Not to worry, there was a taxi rank near the office block. The fare to Parnell and Wilson Wines would be a short one but he'd make it worth the driver's while.

"I want to see Judd Wilson," he demanded as he walked past the reception desk at Wilson Wines about fifteen minutes later.

"Mr. Wilson isn't taking appointments today," the girl behind the desk stated very primly, her expression changing to one of outrage as Nate totally ignored her and started to climb the stairs that led to the management offices of the two-storied building. "Wait, you can't go up there!"

"Just watch me," he said, ascending the stairs two at a time.

At the top of the stairs he caught sight of a woman he recognized as Anna Garrick. Raoul's reporting had been spot-on as usual. The woman was attractive, not unlike Nicole in coloring, but her hair was a little lighter and she was a bit shorter, too.

"Mr. Hunter?" she asked, a startled expression on her face before she pushed it back under a professional facade.

"Where is Wilson? I need to see him."

"Mr. Wilson is still in hospital and visitors are restricted to immediate family only."

"No," he huffed in frustration, "not Charles Wilson, I want to see Judd Wilson, right now."

"Well, then," she said, now appearing completely unruffled. "If you would like to take a seat I'll check if he can see you."

"I'm not waiting. Just show me where he is. This is important."

"Is that so?" Another male voice sounded across the carpeted foyer. "Don't worry, Anna, I'll see him in my office."

Nate couldn't help but intercept the look that passed between the two of them. Questioning his presence, for sure, but there was something more between them. Something that made him feel very much on the outside.

"Where's Nicole?" he demanded, not taking time for introductions or finesse.

"Why don't you come into my office and we'll talk, hmm?"

Judd Wilson gave him a cool blue stare, one that reminded him that he was on their turf right now and in no position to be making demands. With ill-concealed frustration he moved into the room Judd had gestured him into and seated himself in a chair opposite a large mahogany desk. If Jackson Importers was everything that was modern and current, Wilson Wines was the opposite. There was a sense of longevity about the fixtures and fittings, even about the building itself. As if they'd been here awhile and they would be here for quite a while still to come.

The sensation that filled him now was not unlike envy. This should have been part of his father's business, too, part of his legacy. But he didn't have time to dwell on old bitterness and recriminations. Right now he had one priority. Nicole, and her whereabouts.

"Now, how about you tell me what it is you want?" Judd said from the other side of the desk, his gaze still unfriendly.

"Nicole's gone. I need to find out where she went so I can get her back."

"My sister is a big girl now, Hunter. I think if she cannot be reached by you, then perhaps she simply doesn't want to be."

"She's not herself at the moment. She's been under immense pressure and I don't think she's capable of making a rational decision right now. Please, you must help me," Nate implored, shoving pride to one side for the sake of the woman he loved and cared for more than anyone else in the world.

"Must? I don't think so. Not under the circumstances. She left us to be with you. Now she's left you, too. What makes you think we'd do anything to help you get her back?"

"I think she's gone to Adelaide with your mother."

Judd leaned back in his chair, the lift of one brow his only expression of surprise at the news.

"No, she wouldn't have done that," Anna Garrick's voice came from the door.

"Why not?" Nate asked, confused. Nicole had made the point quite clear in her voice message that her mother had invited her to leave New Zealand with her.

"Because she couldn't, that's why. Her passport is still here in the office safe."

Nate felt all the fight drain out of him. Now he had no idea where Nicole could be. Searching for her would be like looking for a needle in a haystack. He had no rights to find out where she was. She'd left on her own accord, severing all ties with him.

"Thank you," he said brokenly, getting up from his seat and making for the door.

"Hunter, can I ask why you're so desperate to find her?" Judd asked from behind the desk.

"Because I love her, and I've done the most stupid thing in my life by letting her go."

# Twelve

The look of shock on Judd's and Anna's faces had been little compensation for the empty days, and nights that stretched ahead. By Friday night Nate was a mess—his concentration shot to pieces, his temper frayed. He'd never been this helpless in his life. Well, at least not since his father's fallout with Charles Wilson, when his whole world had turned upside down.

It didn't help that everything around him reminded him of Nicole. From the lotions and perfume on his bathroom vanity, to the items of clothing that were mixed in with his laundry. Even in the office there was the constant reminder of her phone in his drawer, her laptop neatly sitting on the top of the desk.

Every day since she'd left he'd asked himself where she could be. He'd toyed with reporting her missing to the police, but he was quite certain he'd have been laughed out of the station. After all, she was an adult.

They'd had a fight. The separation that had come next was a natural progression. Except it felt unnatural in every way, shape and form.

Someone had to know where she was. She was a gregarious creature, one who got along with people. A pack animal rather than a loner. He wracked his brains to think of who she could have been in touch with. Only one name came to mind.

Anna Garrick. She'd said very little when he'd been at their office on Tuesday morning. Mind you, he'd been an over-reactive idiot—making demands and being belligerent. Hardly the way to garner respect or assistance. It was possible, too, that Nicole may not have even been in touch with her at that stage, but who was to say she hadn't been in touch since?

The time between making his decision to speak with Anna and arriving at the Wilson home became a blur. As he directed his car up the driveway he couldn't help but admire the enormous replica gothic mansion that loomed at the top. It had taken a hell of lot of hard work to build all of this and then to hold on to it, he knew, and he found himself experiencing a begrudging respect for the man who had held it all together.

He went to the door and lifted the old-fashioned knocker, letting it fall against the brass plate behind it.

A neatly suited man answered the door.

"I'd like to see Ms. Garrick, please," Nate said, after he gave his name.

"One moment please, sir. If you'll just take a seat in the salon, I'll see if she's free."

Nate didn't know if Anna was playing games with him or if she was simply genuinely busy, but he didn't like having to cool his heels for a good twenty minutes before she came into the salon to greet him. He had to remind himself more than once that he needed to keep his impatience in check if he was to find out if she knew where Nicole was.

When she finally deigned to see him she was composed and solicitous, probably more so than he deserved after the last time he'd seen her. She offered him a drink, obviously comfortable in her role as hostess. Nate declined her offer, too filled with nervous energy to do anything but pace the confines of the room. She composed herself on an elegantly covered antique two-seater sofa and eyed him carefully.

"What can I do for you, Mr. Hunter?"

"Nate, please call me Nate."

"Nate, then. What is it that you want?"

He swallowed and chose his words carefully. "Have you heard from Nicole?"

"If I had, do you really think she'd want me to tell you?"

He sighed. "I take it you have, then. Is she—"

"She's fine, but she doesn't want to see you or anyone else right now."

Nate lifted his eyes to Anna's, searching her calm hazel gaze for any sign that she was worried about her friend.

"I need to see her," he said, the words blunt and filled with an edge of pain he couldn't hide.

Anna shook her head. "Isn't it enough to know she's okay?"

"What do you think?" he asked her, letting every raw pain of loss show in his eyes. "I love her, Anna. I have to tell her I'm sorry, and I need to see if she'll give me another chance."

"I would be betraying her trust if I told you where she was. I've already done that once, recently, and I have to tell you that I'm not prepared to do that again. It nearly destroyed our friendship."

"Don't you think I know that? I'm begging you here."

"I can't. She needs to know she can trust me."

Nate felt as if a giant ball of lead had settled in his gut. Anna had been his only hope. "I want her to know she can trust me, too," he said brokenly as he rose to his feet and headed out the room. At the doorway he turned, "Thank you for seeing me. If you talk to her soon, please tell her...ah, hell, don't worry, it wouldn't make a difference, anyway."

The pity in Anna Garrick's eyes cut him straight to his heart. Nicole was lucky to have a friend like her, he told himself as he forced his feet toward the front door and headed down the stairs toward his car.

The heavy tread of rapid footsteps followed him down the stairs.

"Hunter, wait up."

It was Judd Wilson. Nate turned to face him.

"Yeah," he said, without even the will to fake a politeness he certainly didn't feel.

"I know where she is."

Nate felt something leap in his chest. "And you'll tell me?"

"Anna will kill me for this, but someone needs to cut you a break," the other man said. "Anyone can see you're hurting. The two of you need to work this out one way or another. You both deserve that much." He gave Nate an address about a two-hour drive north of Auckland. "Don't make me regret this, Hunter. If you hurt her again, you'll be answering to me."

Nate proffered his hand, and felt an overwhelming

sense of relief when Judd took it. Their shake was brisk and brief. "I owe you," he said solemnly.

"Yes, you do," Judd replied just as gravely. "We can talk about that later."

Nate gave him a nod of assent and headed for his car. He needed to swing by the apartment before driving up to see her. There was something he needed to collect. It was late, but maybe Nicole would still be awake by the time he made it to where she was staying. And if she wasn't, well, then he'd just wait until she was.

Nicole brushed the sand off her feet with an old towel she'd been keeping on the edge of the deck for just that purpose. Late-night walks along the sandy shoreline of Langs Beach had become a habit as she tried to do what she could to exhaust herself into sleep every night.

Since making the decision to leave Nate, and risk the consequences, she'd hardly slept a wink. So far Nate hadn't sent the DVD to her father, she knew that much. Anna had been keeping her up to date on her father's progress and it looked as if he'd turned a corner health-wise. Of course, that could all change if he viewed the thing. And while that preyed on her mind, when she was honest with herself, she knew she wasn't sleeping mostly because she missed Nate. Missed his strength, his solid presence beside her at night.

She sighed as she made her way across the deck, her feet frozen in the frigid night air. She could have worn shoes, probably should have, but she loved the feel of the squeaky white sand beneath her feet and, at this time of night, she could enjoy the sensation completely on her own with only the stars above her for company.

The aged French doors groaned as she opened them to let herself inside the rather decrepit holiday home she'd rented. After she'd left her laptop and the phone Nate had given her at the office, she'd just driven north—stopping only long enough to pay for the toll charge on the Northern Motorway and to pick up a cheap prepaid cell phone from a gas station on the way.

She didn't know what had drawn her to the area, aside from the fact it was near the sea and it was nothing like the west coast beach that Nate's house overlooked. Of course, if her goal had been to avoid reminders of Nate, then she'd failed. She hadn't been able to stop thinking about the man since she'd gotten here.

Nicole secured the door and went through to the kitchen to put on the kettle. Maybe a cup of chamomile tea would make the difference tonight and help her to sleep. She stiffened as she heard the sound of a car's tires rolling along the gravel driveway that led to the house. No one knew she was here but Anna, and she wouldn't have come without calling Nicole first.

The walls of the cottage were thin and she could hear a heavy measured tread come toward the house. A tread that seemed to hesitate on the wooden steps that led to the front door before she heard a solid one-two-three knock on the peeling painted surface.

Her heart hammering in her chest, she moved closer to the front door.

"Nicole, it's me, Nate."

How had he found her? More to the point, now that he had, what was she going to do?

"Nicole, please. I'm not here to hurt you or to argue with you. I just want to talk."

She hesitated a moment before reaching a trembling

hand to the lock at the door and swinging the door open. Shock hit her when she saw him illuminated beneath the bare bulb that lit the front porch. As much as she tried to harden her heart against him, she couldn't help but be concerned at his appearance. He looked as if he hadn't slept or eaten properly in days. Probably much as she looked herself. Except when she looked at him all she wanted to do was comfort him.

She fought against the urge to hold her arms out to him, to offer him respite from the demons that had obviously ridden him this week. Demons that might be similar to those she'd been wrestling with herself—unsuccessfully, too, if her instinctive reaction to him was any indicator. She took a deep breath and forced her hands to stay at her sides.

"You'd better come in," she said stiffly, standing aside and gesturing toward the open-plan living room/kitchen.

The place was basic. One bedroom, one bathroom and everything else all there for anyone to see. The property's saving graces had been its proximity to the beach and a modern lock-up garage where she'd stowed the Mercedes.

"Can I get you a warm drink?"

She didn't want to offer him any alcohol before sending him back on his way again, especially not looking the way he did right now. The last thing she wanted to be responsible for was him having an accident.

"No, thanks," he said, his voice ragged. "How are you, really?"

She poured boiling water over the tea bag in her cup and then took it over to one of the chairs in the lounge. Nate sat down on the sofa opposite.

"I'm okay. Look, I don't know why you're here but you won't change my mind. I meant what I said in my message."

Nate reached inside his jacket pocket and took out a flat case. A case she recognized with dread. He tried to hand it over to her and when she didn't take it—she couldn't risk touching him—he placed it on the scarred coffee table between them. She could see her refusal to take the case had surprised him, perhaps even hurt him.

She looked at the case, lying there, inert on the tabletop. So seemingly nondescript, yet so potentially damaging at the same time.

"It's yours," he said.

"What? A copy?"

"The only copy," he said, lifting his face so his eyes met hers. "I couldn't send it to your father—I couldn't do that to you, Nicole. I want you to know that. I could never hurt you like that. I know I threatened to, more than once. But even if I hadn't fallen in love with you I couldn't have abused your trust of me that way."

A fist clenched tight around her heart. Had she heard him right? Or was this just another ploy to get her back where he wanted her?

"You seemed pretty determined. Why should I believe you've changed your mind now?"

The voice that came from her mouth didn't sound like her at all. It was harsh, unforgiving.

He hung his head. "I don't deserve for you to believe me but I hope that you can find your way clear to understand where I'm coming from." He lifted his head again, his eyes filled with anguish. "I know I've been a total monster. I should have told you from the beginning who I was. I should have left you in the bar that night. But I couldn't. Even then I was compelled to be with you. I wanted you and I had to have you."

Nicole gripped her mug tight, mindless to the heat that stung her fingers. Just hearing him say the words about wanting her had her body beginning to light up in response. The old familiar coil of desire tightening deep inside her, craving his touch. Craving him.

"And once you had me, you used me," she said bitterly.

"I'm sorry. I know it sounds trite and empty and worthless, but please believe me. I am so sorry I treated you that way. If I had the chance again I would do everything differently."

And so would she, Nicole thought. For a start she wouldn't have left the house that night. Wouldn't have stormed away and wouldn't have lost herself in the one man who could hurt her more than any other. The man she'd fallen painfully in love with. Her heart beat faster in her chest as she acknowledged the painful truth for what it was. Hopeless. She couldn't trust him. He was a master at manipulation, he'd borne a grudge against her father for most of his life. How could she even begin to believe his words were anything more than another tool to control her?

"Is that everything?" she asked coolly. She held her body so rigid that she was afraid she'd shatter into a million pieces if he so much as reached across the table and touched her.

"No, it's not everything. I could spend the rest of my life telling you how much I regret treating you so badly and it would never be long enough. I love you, Nicole. I'm ashamed that I had to lose you to admit it to myself, but there you have it. On the beach that day I asked you to marry me. I'd fooled myself into thinking it was for the baby's sake, and hurt you by asking you for all the wrong reasons when I should have just asked you for you. Will you give me another chance? Let me make it up to you. Let me love you the way you deserve to be loved."

Nicole shook her head. It was a slight movement but Nate saw it and recognized it for what it was. He tried one more time.

"Please, don't make your mind up right now. Give it a few more days. Come back to the city, come back to me. Let's try again and this time I promise I'll get it right."

"No," she said, feeling as if her heart would break with verbalizing that one syllable. "I can't, Nate. I can't trust you not to hurt me like that again. Me or my family. I just can't." And she couldn't trust herself, either. She loved him too much. If she went back, if she let herself be with him again, she'd find herself falling back into his plans, for better or for worse. And she wasn't going to do that again.

Nate looked at her for a full minute, her words hanging in the air between them like an impenetrable shield. Then, slowly he nodded and rose from the sofa. She didn't move as he crossed the room and moved down the short hall toward the front door. It wasn't until she heard the snick of the lock as the door reseated in its frame behind him, that the shudders began to rack her body and the sobs rose from deep within.

He was gone. She'd sent him away. It was what she wanted, wasn't it?

Nate walked to his car wrapped in a blanket of numbness. She'd refused him. It was his worst-case scenario come to living, breathing, painful, life. He settled behind the wheel of the Maserati, and switched the wipers on only to turn them off again as they scraped across the dry windscreen. It was only then he realized the moisture he felt on his face had not been from any rain outside, but from his own tears.

He started the car and eased it up the driveway, away from the house, away from Nicole, swiping at his cheeks and eyes as he did so. He felt as if he was leaving his soul behind, as if he was just a shell now. An empty shell. She'd completed him and he hadn't even had the good sense to know it or appreciate it until it was too late.

At the top of the driveway he looked back, hoping against hope that she might be silhouetted in the doorway, that she might beckon to him to come back. If she did, then together they could find a way to work past the damage he'd wrought. Instead, he saw the outside light extinguish, and with it his last remaining hope.

He blinked hard. He'd lost her. He'd abused her trust, he'd threatened her family. He had gotten exactly what he deserved.

Nate turned the car onto the winding road that would eventually lead him back to State Highway One, back to Auckland. Back to a life lived alone with his grand, empty plans for revenge.

His eyes burned in their sockets by the time he crossed the Auckland Harbor Bridge and turned off toward the Viaduct Basin. Weariness dragged at his body as he let himself into the apartment, a place that felt empty without Nicole inside. As exhausted as he was, sleep was the last thing on his mind. Somehow he had to find a way to convince Nicole she could trust him and that his love for her was real. There had to be a way, there just had to be, because he couldn't imagine the rest of his life without her by his side.

It simply wasn't an option.

# Thirteen

Nate straightened from his car outside the Wilson family home. He hadn't slept all night and was running on pure adrenaline right now. He hammered at the front door and stood back in the portico waiting for someone to respond.

It took a while but eventually the door swung open to reveal Judd Wilson dressed in pajama bottoms and a robe. His hair was rumpled, as if he'd run his fingers through it in an attempt to tidy it before answering the door.

"Good grief, man, have you any idea what time it is?" he grumbled at Nate.

"Look, I know it's early but I had to talk to you. This is too important to wait."

"You'd better come in, then." Judd gave him a hard look. "Have you seen yourself this morning?"

Nate grimaced in response. He knew he looked

about as rough as he felt. He hadn't shaved or combed his hair and he was still in the clothing he'd worn last night.

"Judd? Who is it?" Anna's voice came from the top of the staircase.

"It's Nate Hunter."

"And Nicole? Is she all right?"

Anna came down the stairs, a dressing gown wrapped about her and tied with a sash at her waist.

"Nicole was fine when I left her," Nate ground out. "She doesn't want a bar of me but I'm hoping that we can change that, together."

Judd and Anna exchanged a look before Judd spoke. "You need to fight your own battles, Hunter. My sister is responsible for her own choices."

"I know, but I have a proposal I think you might find worth listening to. Something that will benefit you and Wilson Wines, and that just might show Nicole how much I care."

"Sounds like something best done on a full stomach with a decent cup of coffee inside you," Anna said. "Judd?"

"Sure, come through to the kitchen," Judd agreed.

"We gave our house staff the weekend off, so I hope you don't mind if things are a little more basic than we can usually offer," Anna said as she pushed open the swing doors that led into the spacious modernized kitchen.

"Food is the least of my worries," Nate said, lowering himself into one of the kitchen chairs and pulling a sheaf of papers from his coat pocket. "Please don't go to any bother on my account."

As Anna began to make coffee, Nate started to outline his plan. Judd remained silent through most of it, only stopping Nate every now and then to ask him to clarify one point or another. By the time Anna slid plates of French toast and bacon in front of them both, and topped up their coffees, he was wrapping up.

"So, to sum it all up, I suggest that we amalgamate Jackson Importers and Wilson Wines and go forward as one powerful entity for the future, rather than two companies, which are absorbed in competing with one another. It's how it was meant to be all along, it's up to us to make it that way again."

"Why?" Judd asked. "I mean, the idea is definitely worth exploring, but why now?"

"Because I don't see why we should continue to be victims of our fathers' falling out."

"Your fathers?" Anna asked. "You're—?"

"Yes, I'm Thomas Jackson's son."

Judd leaned back in his chair and gave Nate a hard look. "You're certain you want to do this?"

"I've never been more certain of anything in my life," Nate said emphatically.

"You realize I can't do anything without discussing this with my father and with Nicole."

"I understand that. If possible, I'd like to be there when you talk to your father. I think it's time that the past be firmly put to bed. That all the bitterness be dissolved once and for all. It's hurt too many people for too long. It has to stop."

Nicole missed Nate with an ache that went painfully deep. Nights were fractured with dreams of him, days were filled with trying to forget him. But try as she might, she failed miserably. If only they could have met under normal circumstances, without the stupid feud between their families. If only she could trust that he loved her for herself and not out of some twisted sense of revenge. A person didn't let go of that much animosity easily.

She'd thought that getting away from him, getting away from the city would help. But it hadn't helped a bit. If anything it had only served to magnify her feelings for him. Without anything else to distract her, he was all she could think about. Especially after he told her he loved her—and she'd had to send him away.

Maybe she should get a dog, she pondered as she sat on the deck outside the cottage in the watery sunshine and watched a local resident throwing a stick for his dog on the beach. Even as she considered it she knew it couldn't replace the hole in her heart loving Nate had left. Loving him? How could she love him? He'd virtually kidnapped her, had held her against her will, had forced her to work with him instead of where she rightfully belonged. She made a mental note to look up Stockholm syndrome as soon as she could access a computer. She had to find some reason for this irrational attachment to the man.

But was it so irrational? Their attraction that night at the bar had been mutual and instant. Fierce. At least it had been on her side. His? Well, the jury was still out on that one. He'd been following an agenda, hadn't he?

Seeing him last night was tough. Had their circumstances been any different, had he not been so bent on revenge for what her father had done, she'd have dragged him to the tiny bedroom and laid him bare upon the covers of the double bed and taken her time in punishing him slowly for his behavior.

Her body flushed with heat at the thought. Heat that was rapidly diminished by the cool breeze coming in off the ocean. Exercise, she needed exercise. Anything to wear her out and distract her from her thoughts. She grabbed her puffy jacket from inside the cottage and pulled on a pair of sneakers before heading north up the beach. The wind had risen by the time she reached the end and started to walk back, bringing with it the scent of rain.

By the time she got to the cottage the rain was driving across the sand. She hastened inside, taking her jacket off in the tiny bathroom and hanging it over the shower rail to dry. Making her way to the kitchen, she put on the kettle for a warming cup of tea, as she did so she noticed her phone flashing that she had a message.

Not just one message. Several. And several missed calls, as well. All of them from Anna. What could be so important on a Saturday morning? she wondered. She knew it wasn't her father. He was making steady progress at the hospital and they were even talking about him coming home soon. Dialysis would be a major part of his future but at least he had a future. The messages were all the same—Anna asking Nicole to call her back right away. Her friend sounded excited, but not upset, Nicole noted. She poured her cup of tea and took the cup and her phone over to the sofa where Nate had sat last night, the stuffing so worn that the imprint of his body was still there.

Before she could stop herself, Nicole reached a hand to where he'd been sitting, as if she could somehow sense the man in the impression he'd left behind. A particularly strong gust of wind drove against the beachside windows of the house, making her jump and shaking her from her reverie. She had a call to make. She didn't need to be thinking about Nate. Not now, not ever.

Anna answered the phone on the first ring. "Nic, Judd needs to speak to you. Hold on and I'll put him on."

Judd's warm deep voice filled her ear. "How's it going?"

"It's okay. The weather's rubbish but aside from that I'm doing all right." Ironic, she thought, one of the few conversations she should have with her brother and it should be about the weather.

"Glad to hear it. Look, I'll cut to the chase. I have some important Wilson Wines business to discuss with you but I don't want to do it over the phone. Can you come into the office on Monday? I'd really rather do this face-to-face."

Monday? She could do that. It wasn't as if she had any other pressing social engagements on her calendar, she thought cynically.

"Sure, what time?"

"Let's say eleven. That should give you plenty of time to get down here, shouldn't it?"

"I'll be there."

Judd wasted no further time on any pleasantries, severing the call almost immediately after her confirmation. Well, it wasn't as if they had a normal brother-sister relationship. They hadn't ever had the chance. She wondered what it was he wanted to discuss. Hopefully it would have something to do with her coming back to Wilson Wines and reassuming her position there. Then, maybe, she could undo some of the damage she'd done with her work for Jackson Importers.

Monday morning rolled around slowly and Nicole was on the road earlier than she needed be. After an-

other night plagued with dreams of Nate, she couldn't
wait to have something else to distract her. The traffic
heading into Auckland was that and then some.

Pulling into her usual car park at Wilson Wines felt
strange, but that was nothing to what it felt like walking back into the building. Everything was still exactly the same. She didn't know why she'd expected it
to have changed in any way, except that she had been
through so much since the last time she'd been here
that she felt that time should have marked its passage
here somehow.

Their receptionist told her to go on upstairs and that
Judd was waiting for her. Anna met her at the top of
the stairs and gave her a quick hug.

"Do you know what this is about?" Nicole asked.

"It's better you hear it from Judd," she said with a
smile. "He's waiting in your dad's old office."

"Old office? So he's not coming back?"

"It's unlikely. Even though he's a lot better he's not
up to the day-to-day demands of business anymore."

Nicole was shocked. Her father had always been invincible. A powerhouse. They'd butted heads over his
unwillingness to accept her ideas for advancement but,
that said, she couldn't imagine the company without
her father at the helm.

"Is that what Judd wants to talk to me about?"

"Go and see him," was all Anna would say.

Squaring her shoulders, Nicole walked toward her
father's office. Judd's office, now, she supposed. He
got up from behind the desk when she knocked and
pushed open the door.

"I'm glad you could come," he said, first holding out
his hand and then drawing her into his arms for a swift

embrace. "We haven't exactly been able to get off to a good start, have we?"

"No," Nicole said, a nervous smile on her face. Considering she'd pretty much been pouting like a spoiled brat when he'd arrived, followed a few days later by her storming out of the house, his comment was a mastery of understatement.

"Hopefully we can amend that, if you're willing?"

"Sure. Who knows, we might even like each other."

Judd flashed her a smile and in it she could see a hint of their father's humor. It made her instantly feel more comfortable with him. It was a comfort she clung to as he started to talk about what he'd asked her in to discuss.

"You mean this was Nate's idea? That he *wants* to amalgamate the businesses?"

She got up from her seat and walked over to the window that looked out over the city. Nate? Merge Jackson Importers with Wilson Wines? What ever happened to his passion for revenge? By his own admission it had driven him since he was a child. Why stop now? They both knew that the deal was to Wilson Wines's advantage. The company was in a weakened managerial position with Judd inexperienced with the firm and her father incapable of reassuming his role. If Jackson Importers wanted to put them out of business, now was the time. Why was Nate throwing them a lifeline, instead?

"It was his idea, and after discussing it with him and going over the figures, I'm inclined to accept. It makes sense. Not only that, but it closes a door that's been open too long. It gives both our families a chance to heal."

Nicole shook her head. She couldn't believe it. "Are

you sure he doesn't have some ulterior motive behind this?"

"We stand to gain far more than he does at the moment. I'm sure you're even more aware of that than he is. You've worked with him. You know how strong they are in the marketplace, here and overseas. He's done that. With him running the whole company, they're poised to grow even stronger. Of course, Wilson Wines brings a respected name and established reputation to the table—but unless we modernize and expand, our company will grow weaker while his grows stronger. This is just what we need to get back on track."

She sat back down in her seat. Could Nate have been telling the truth when he came to see her on Friday night? Was he really letting all that resentment and hostility toward her family go, just like that? Was this a chance to finally mend the gaping rifts in her family life and allow her to feel whole again?

Was this the chance for her and Nate, after all?

"And you want an opinion from me today? Really, I need some time to think about this," she said.

"Look, I know it's a lot to take in. Goodness only knows Anna and I have made the most of having the past couple of days to begin to get used to the idea. But it's not just my decision to make. It affects you, as well."

Nicole felt the old acrimony rise in her throat again. "No, it doesn't. You have the controlling share in Wilson Wines. Dad holds the balance. It's your decision, Judd, whether you want that or not."

Judd lifted an envelope from the top of the desk and handed it to her. "Here, maybe what's inside will help you make up your mind."

She took the envelope. "What is it?"

He laughed. "Nothing that'll hurt you, Nicole. Seriously, just open it."

She slid a nail under the flap and ripped the envelope open. Inside was a single sheet of paper. A company share transfer, to be exact. Her eyes widened as she read the terms of the transfer. Judd was giving her everything their father had given him. Not half, not less than half. All of it. If she signed this paper she would have the controlling share and the decision as to how Wilson Wines would go forward.

"Have you lost your mind?" she asked.

"No, if anything I've found it. I learned the hard way that a life bent on revenge is no life at all. I think that Nate has recently discovered much the same thing. I nearly lost Anna over my need to make our father pay for abandoning me and our mother. For denying me my birthright until it suited him to get Anna to bring me back. I don't want to lose out on anything else. Neither does Nate.

"We've all been hurt, Nicole. But we deserve to be happy—*really* happy. I know I'm doing the right thing in giving this to you and I know you'll do the right thing in return."

"And are you happy now, Judd?"

"With Anna, yes. I'm going to marry her, Nicole. I know you two are close and I want you to know I'm going to look after her."

Nicole sat back in her chair and looked at him, and smiled again. Her first genuine smile since she'd arrived today. Maybe her first genuine smile in a long, long time. "You'd better, or you'll answer to me."

"Noted," he said with a nod. "Now, how about you take the next day or so to think about things? Anna

has a folder ready for you to take with you so you can
analyze Nate's proposal in depth."

Nicole sat in her car in the car park still shocked by
the news Judd had given her today, especially his intention to marry her best friend. When pressed, Anna
had admitted her love for Judd in return, but said they
weren't going to make a public announcement until
Charles was home and settled again. They'd already
sought his blessing, which had been rapidly forthcom-
ing, apparently. Which left Nicole exactly where?

She had plenty to think about, she realized as
she started the car and backed out of the car space.
It wasn't until she'd headed for the motorway interchange that would lead her back up north that she made
a sudden decision to turn around and drive back the
way she'd come.

The Auckland City Hospital car park was pretty
empty given the time of day, and it didn't take her
long to find a space. In no time she was in an elevator,
heading for her father's ward. She only hoped that he'd
agree to see her. If, as Judd had said, they all deserved
happiness, then it was time for some truths between
her and her father, especially the truth about her more
recent behavior. Only with everything out in the open
could the wounds—both old and more recent—finally
heal.

She fought to hide her shock when she saw him
lying against his pillows, his eyes closed. The ravages
of illness had made him lose a great deal of weight
and his skin held an unhealthy pallor. She could have
lost him. Would have never had the chance to make
amends. And all for what?

"Dad?" she said tentatively as she closed the door to the private room behind her.

His eyes shot open and Nicole was relieved to see they were full of their usual fiery intelligence.

"You came back."

His tone of voice gave nothing away but she caught the telltale tremor around his mouth. And was that a hint of moisture in his eyes?

"Oh, Dad. Of course I came back. I miss you."

"Ah, my little girl. Come here," he said, his voice shaking as he parted the side of the bed and opened his arms.

Nicole shifted to his side and let herself be enveloped by his hug, mindful of the monitors and tubes he was still attached to. But all that was peripheral to the fact that she was here, that he hadn't sent her away again.

"I've missed you, too. I've had plenty of time to think, lately, and I know I owe you an apology. Several apologies, actually."

"No, Dad, it's okay," she protested. "I've always acted first, thought second. I should have stayed. We'd have worked it out."

"No, it's not okay. I never gave you a fair shot, did I? I was so angry with you for defecting to the enemy after Judd came home that the sight of you in the emergency department just made me see red. But I was wrong. When all is said and done, family comes first. I should never have pushed you away in the first place. I should have included you when I decided to approach Judd about coming back home. It was wrong of me to make those decisions, decisions that affected you, without any consultation as a family."

"It's okay, Dad, I understand. It hurt me, but I do

understand. You never got the chance to raise Judd the way you wanted to. All of that was stolen from you."

"Stolen with a single lie," he said sadly. "Did you know that? Your mother told me Judd wasn't my son. To my shame I believed her and when she named my best friend as Judd's father, I stupidly believed that, too. So many years lost, so much time wasted."

"But you can make up for that now," she urged, shocked at the way his body trembled and happier than ever that she had chosen not to run away from her problems to Australia with Cynthia. She did want to meet her family at some point—get to know her cousins and uncles and aunts, but cementing things with her family here took priority.

"For what time I have left," Charles replied. "You know, Nicole, pride is a terrible thing. Because of pride I lost my wife, my son, my best friend and my health. If I had my time over again, I'd do so much differently. Maybe then I could have been the husband Cynthia needed. I've made some bad decisions in my life, not least of which with you.

"I know you think I was holding you back at Wilson Wines and, yes, I suppose I was. But I could just see so much of myself in you. You were so driven, so determined to grow the business to the exception of everything else in your life. I've always wanted the best for you but when I saw you going down the same road that I went, I had to do something to hold you back. You deserve more than just a business. You deserve a life enriched with a husband and children and steadiness at home—not all your energy driven into work and serving the mighty dollar as I have done."

"But I love my work at Wilson Wines, Dad. I've missed it."

"I thought limiting your requirements at work would push you to invest more of your time and energy into relationships. I shouldn't have made that decision for you. I'll wager you had more freedom with that Nate Hunter than you had with me. Don't bother denying it. He saw a good thing and he took advantage of it."

"Dad, there's something you should know about him."

"Beyond the fact he's a fearsome business opponent? Can't help but admire him for that, if nothing else."

She didn't know how to phrase this carefully, so she just came out with it. "He's Thomas's son."

Her father closed his eyes briefly before giving a deep sigh. "That explains a lot," he said quietly. "Another life harmed. Clearly I owe him an apology, too. It can't have been easy for him growing up. Are the two of you an item?"

Nicole shook her head. "We were. But I ended it. He wanted me for all the wrong reasons."

"And what are those?" Charles urged.

"Revenge against you, for one thing," she admitted. It sounded so pathetic when she put it into words to the man it had been directed against. But that's pretty much what it all came down to in the end, wasn't it?

Charles chuckled. "A chip off the old block, hmm? Well, I can't say I blame him. He had just cause."

Nicole could barely believe her ears. All his life her father had spoken in derogatory terms about Thomas Jackson and now he laughed about Nate's vendetta?

"Aren't you angry?"

"Not anymore," he said with a deep sigh. "There's a lot to be said for facing your mortality. It makes you see things differently."

"Judd gave me his controlling share of the company," she blurted.

"Did he? Well, that was his choice to make. I should never have created such a divisive position between you two but it was so important to me to bring Judd home, and I really did want to force you to create some balance in your life."

By the time she left the hospital it was growing late. Despite a few dark looks from the nursing staff, she'd been allowed to stay at her father's side all afternoon and they'd talked to one another as they'd never talked before. As she clipped her seatbelt across her chest she recognized that the feeling inside her now was one of happiness and acceptance of her position in her father's heart. She held all the cards now. She was no longer a pawn, she was the player.

Which left her only one last thing to do.

# Fourteen

Her headlights picked out the possum ahead of her on the winding curve of road. Thankfully she avoided it without incident and could focus her attention to the confrontation she had ahead. Nate hadn't been at the office when she'd called, nor had he been at the apartment when she'd stopped in there. Which only left the beach house.

How appropriate that this would end where it had begun.

She cruised through the bends in the dark ribbon of tarseal slowly, more familiar with being a passenger on the journey than the driver. It was an interesting analogy for her life. Despite her efforts to get ahead and to be noticed in her life, she'd always allowed herself to be acted upon rather than to take charge and be fully responsible for her own behavior.

The idea that she was free of her previous constraints, constraints she'd allowed even into adulthood, was intensely liberating. Even so, she felt as if hummingbirds danced in her stomach as she neared the driveway to Nate's house. She pulled up outside the garage door and walked around to the main entrance, pressing the door bell several times in quick succession.

The door opened.

"Nicole!"

Nate looked stunned to see her, but she felt his eyes roam her as if he were touching her. Her traitorous body responded in kind. She dropped her eyes from his, hoping he hadn't seen her reaction reflected in her gaze.

"We need to talk," she said brusquely. "May I come in?"

He stood aside and gestured for her to take a seat in the living room. "Can I get you anything?" he offered.

"This isn't a social visit," she said firmly. It was important to her that she set the parameters right from the start. "I need to know something."

"Ask me. I'll tell you whatever I can."

"Are you still playing some game with my family with your proposal to join the companies together?"

He looked surprised. "You know about that already?"

"Judd called me down from Langs Beach to discuss it. He's given me a written report, which I haven't read yet. I needed to talk to you first so I can decide whether to read it, or whether to use it to light a fire, instead."

He gave a disparaging laugh. "It's not a game—it's anything but."

"So this is really what you want?"

He looked her square in the eye and she could see

the truth burning there in those sherry-brown depths. "Yes."

"And you're not doing this to somehow undermine my family or to hurt them?"

"No, I'm not."

She took a deep breath. "Or to hurt me?"

"Never to hurt you, Nicole. That was *never* my intention. I wanted to give you every opportunity to succeed all along."

"Why are you doing this, then?"

Nate sighed and leaned forward, resting his elbows on his thighs and clasping his capable hands in front of him. His gaze was fixed on her face, as if he was willing her to believe him.

"I made the suggestion for three very good reasons. The first is that it makes sound business sense. If we stop competing with one another we'll be in a stronger position when it comes to securing new business—one less player in the market should give us an edge on pricing. It's all in the report, when you read it you'll see what I'm talking about."

Nicole nodded. "Okay, so that's one reason. What about the others?"

"It was time to stop the feud. It's hurt too many people for too long. One of us had to make the first move. I decided it was time for me to let go of my grudge. Sure, I had a tough upbringing, a lot of kids did. I still had more advantages than most. Even while my mother and I were living hand to mouth my father was ensuring that I still had the best education that he could provide for me. And having to struggle a little made me tough, it made me determined. It made me the man I am today. Flawed, sure, but I know what's right, and letting go of the anger, letting go of the pain—it all had to happen so we can move forward.

"Pride can be a killer. I didn't want it to destroy every last thing I held dear."

Nicole nodded. Hadn't her father spoken along the same lines? She said as much to Nate.

He nodded gently. "You know, I want to see him if he's agreeable. We have a lot to talk about."

"I think he'd like that. I told him today about you. I was sure he was going to tell me that he'd be quite happy to carry on the competition between Wilson Wines and Jackson Importers indefinitely, but this latest illness has changed him, too. It's altered his perspective on things."

She paused for a moment, reflecting on the things her father had said, then reminded herself she was here for a reason. "What's the third reason?" Nicole pushed.

"The third reason? You already know that one."

She looked at him, puzzled. She already knew? When she said nothing, Nate continued.

"I love you."

"That's it?" She felt her skepticism rise.

"Yeah, that's it," he said with a deprecating chuckle. "Although I never quite expected to get that response."

"That's not what I mean—" she started to protest, but he cut her off.

"Nicole, I knew that after what I'd put you through, for you to believe that I love you would take an action on my part to prove it, beyond any shadow of a doubt. And I was already working at a disadvantage, because of the mistakes I'd made in our relationship. When I asked you to marry me on the beach out here, when I thought you were carrying my baby, I was prepared to do whatever I could to protect you and provide for you and our child, but I know I went about it all wrong. You have to understand. I grew up illegitimate. Sure, I know that wasn't the worst thing that could happen to me and I certainly wasn't the only kid in class from a single-parent family—but I wanted more for my child than I had."

He got up and began to pace the room, shoving his hands through his hair and sending it into disarray before pushing them deep into the pockets of his trousers. Nicole could see the outlines of his fists through the fine wool of his pants, could sense the tension in every line of his body.

"Go on," she urged softly. "Tell me the rest."

He stood where he was, staring out the window toward the dark shoreline, to where the moon and stars lit the foam of the waves that curled and raced inexorably onto the sand.

"I wanted to ensure that my child never wanted for anything the way I wanted, but at the same time I wanted him or her to know they were loved. You see, even though we struggled, even though I had to put up with the bullying at school because I was different—because my mother was seen shopping at the local thrift store or because one of the boys' mothers delivered our food parcels while doing her bit for the community—through all that I always knew I was loved. Always. I will never be an absentee father to my children. I will be a part of their lives and I will be there when they need me."

Nate turned and faced Nicole again. "That's the way I love, Nicole. With everything I am. It's the way I love you. I asked you to marry me without even fully understanding just how much a man could love a woman, but I learned that, and more, when you left me. You're everything to me and I knew that I had to prove that to you, even if it meant letting go of everything I'd always believed while I was growing up.

"That's it. I love you. Pure and simple."

Nicole sat there, stunned. What he'd just told her was anything but pure and simple. It showed the depths of the man before her. The man she'd rejected and who hadn't given up.

This wasn't the same person who'd calculatedly brought her back here on that fateful night just over a month ago, a man who was prepared to blackmail her over an illicit weekend of wild pleasure just to hurt her father. He'd changed. The old Nate would never have dreamed of combining their two businesses together to form one perfectly strong whole.

This was a man who loved her. Truly loved her. And she'd changed, too, into someone who wasn't afraid to love him back. She pushed herself to her feet and moved to stand in front of him.

"I believe you," she whispered, her voice shaking with the depth of her own love for him. A love she could finally acknowledge to both herself and to Nate. She raised one hand and cupped his cheek. "I love you, too."

The sound he made was part human and part something else. He turned his face into her hand, pressing his lips against her palm.

"It's more than I deserve," he said brokenly.

"We deserve each other. We're neither of us perfect, but together, maybe we can cancel out the bad and be nothing but good. Love me, Nate. Love me forever."

"You can count on it."

He pulled his hands from his pockets and swooped her up into his arms, carrying her to the bedroom where they'd already created so many special memories. This time they undressed one another slowly, painstakingly—taking their time to kiss and caress every part of each other as they bared skin. As if it was their first time—a voyage of discovery.

When neither of them could wait any longer, Nate covered her body with his own, pausing only to reach for a condom. Nicole stayed his hand.

"No condom," she said. "I want whatever naturally comes next in our lives and I don't want any more barriers between us."

"Are you sure?" he asked, his body rigid beneath her hands as she stroked his buttocks with a featherlight touch and then traced her fingers up the muscles that bracketed his spine. She relished the strength of him, loved that he was all hers.

"Certain," she whispered as she lifted her mouth to his, claiming his lips in a kiss that imbued everything she felt at that moment, and when he slid inside her she knew she'd made the right decision. Nothing had ever felt as good as this contact between them, heat to heat, nothing but him and her.

Nate started to move and she met him, stroke for stroke, her cries of pleasure intensifying as he pushed them over the edge of sanity and into another realm where only the two of them existed.

Afterward, they lay still locked together as one. As their breathing slowed and returned to something approaching normal, Nicole lifted a hand and traced the outline of Nate's face. He had never been more precious to her than he was at this moment.

"Do you think we'd have ended up like this without our parents' falling out?"

Nate smiled. "Who knows? I'd like to think so. I

202   A FORBIDDEN AFFAIR

know there's no one out there in this world for me, but you."

She snuggled against him. "Why do you think she did it?"

"She?"

"My mother. Why do you think she lied to my father for all those years? She drove a wedge between everyone without a second thought."

"You know that for sure?"

"Dad didn't tell me all of it, but he did say that her lie was responsible for what happened."

Nate shifted onto his back, pulling Nicole with him. "I suspected she instigated it all. I couldn't imagine anyone else but her having that power over them. Maybe she resented the time Charles put into the business—who knows—but it's no wonder he reacted the way he did to what he perceived as the ultimate betrayal from his best friend."

"But for her to have let it go on this long...I just don't understand it. Why would she do that?"

Nate closed his arms around Nicole and held her tight against him, making a silent vow that nothing would ever separate them again. "She was obviously a very unhappy woman. I'm sorry she never got to have what we have, but we can't let her spoil it for us, either."

Nate pressed a kiss to the top of Nicole's head. "I'm so sorry for everything I did to you, Nicole. I kidded myself that if I gave you everything I thought you wanted that you'd be happy to stay with me. I should have realized you deserved so much more."

"Good thing you got it right this time, then, hmm?" Nicole murmured as she shifted and raised herself above him. "Because I'm going to expect a whole lot of this loving."

"I think I'm man enough for the job." He smiled from beneath her, his body hardening inside her as she rocked gently against him. He gripped her hips with his hands, stilling her motion and his eyes grew serious. "Nicole, I mean it, though. Can you forgive what I did to you?"

"Of course I can, Nate. I already have. We both did things we regret."

"There's one thing I'll never regret," he said, continuing to hold her still. "And that's meeting you. You taught me to open my eyes and to love with all my heart. No conditions, no strings. You will marry me, won't you?"

"Yes," she replied. "I love you, Nate Hunter Jackson, and I will marry you."

"That's good," he replied, "because I'd hate to have to kidnap you all over again."

She laughed, her inner muscles tightening around him as she did so. She'd never felt this happy, or this complete before in her life. She belonged with him, as he did with her. All the security, love and recognition she'd craved all her life lay here with this incredibly special man. Their road together hadn't been smooth so far, but nothing worthwhile in life came easily. She knew that to the very depths of her soul. She also knew she loved him, and that her future would be all the better for having him at her side.

\* \* \* \* \*

# FOR LOVE OR MONEY
## Elizabeth Bevarly

# One

Dinah's fingers convulsed on the telephone. For once in her life, luck seemed to be on her side. Maybe moving to San Francisco hadn't been such a bad idea, after all.

The lottery ticket she was holding in her hand had come to her attention while sorting through all those as-yet-unpacked boxes that had been stacked in her spare room since moving from Atlanta three months before.

In hindsight she supposed it would have made sense to call about the tickets *before* she'd left Georgia— after all, some of them had been months old when she moved. But it had never really occurred to her that one of them might have been a winning combination. Who ever really thought they'd win the lottery?

Still, she must have some deeply buried optimistic streak if she'd packed the tickets along with the other nonessential odds and ends from her kitchen, instead of tossing them out. That same streak must have caused her to call the toll-free number to double check—just in case—instead of throwing the tickets into the garbage with all the obsolete business cards and expired coupons amid which they'd been mingling.

Funny, her being a closet optimist, Dinah thought. Her family did, after all, carry the infamous Curse of the Meades.

"So how many of the numbers did I get right?" she asked the Georgia Lottery representative on the other end of the line. Her fingers trembled now as she threaded them through her straight, pale blond bangs.

If she'd gotten three of the six, she'd won enough to treat herself to a nice dinner, she thought. That might be nice. She could take Marcus. And if she'd matched four numbers, she might just cover a month's rent, which would be *really* nice. And if she'd matched *five*—which she dared not even wish for, because that would be asking too much—Dinah could clear a few thousand dollars. Oh, what a luxury *that* would be. She crossed her fingers as she waited to hear.

From nearly a continent away, the woman from the Georgia Lottery told her, "No, Ms. Meade, you don't understand. I mean you picked some winning numbers. *All* the winning numbers. You've just made yourself a cool five million dollars."

*Thunk.*

It took Dinah a moment to realize it was the phone that had made the sound as it hit the floor and not her head. Though she *had* landed on her fanny when her knees buckled beneath her. *Five million dollars?* she repeated to herself. *Five million dollars?*

*Five Million Dollars!*

"Yes, ma'am. Five million dollars."

Only when she heard the fuzzy reply did Dinah realize she must have shrieked that last one out loud. Even so, the voice reassuring her seemed to be coming from a million miles away. Or, at the very least, three feet away, because that was how far the cordless phone had skittered when it slipped from Dinah's fingers.

Hastily, she scrambled across the kitchen floor on her hands and knees and jerked the phone back up to her ear.

"Are you sure?" she asked the woman. She repeated the numbers again for verification.

"That's the winning combination," the woman assured her. "We thought you'd never come forward."

Dinah recalled her bad habit of buying tickets and magnetting them to the fridge, then forgetting about them. Thank goodness her move had made her check the tickets!

"But as long as you're at lottery headquarters in Atlanta by closing on Monday," the woman said, "you'll collect your money with no problem."

Dinah halted mid-vow. Monday. That was only three days away. And Georgia was…well, more than three days away. At least it was if she drove the distance alone by car or took a train. It would be even longer by bus. But those were her only travel options. No way was she getting on an airplane.

"I'll be there," she reiterated firmly.

She scribbled down the instructions, then hung up the phone. Holy moly. She was a millionaire. Or, at least, she would be. In three days. If she made it back to Georgia in time. And, of course, she *would* make it back to Georgia in time.

She hoped.

A millionaire, she thought again, still numb from the news. She had to tell someone. She had to call someone. She had to shout it to the world. She had to—

A familiar sound out in the hallway caught her attention then, and hastily, she unbolted her back door and jerked it open wide. And when she did, her across-the-hall neighbor, Marcus Harrod, jumped about a foot in the air.

As he always did when returning home from work, he looked like a walking/talking advertisement from *GQ,* wearing a flawless charcoal suit, crisp white dress shirt and expertly knotted and discreetly printed Hermès tie.

Dinah bit back a wistful sigh when she noted how perfectly his attire complemented his silky black hair and luminous blue eyes. He smelled marvelous, looked fabulous, made her little heart go pitter-patter, pitter-patter, pitter-patter. Too bad he wasn't her type. Or more correctly, too bad she wasn't his type.

Damn. All of the good ones were taken. Or else all the good ones were gay.

When he saw that it was Dinah, Marcus fell back against his own door and expelled a gasp of relief. "Jeez, Dinah. I hate it when you do that. You nearly gave me a coronary."

"Marcus!" she cried, ignoring his condition. "I have got the most unbelievable news to tell you!"

"Okay, Dinah, let me get this straight."

Marcus Harrod tipped the bottle of single-malt Scotch over a cut crystal tumbler and tried to digest everything his across-the-hall neighbor—and the object of most of his sexual fantasies these days—had just told him.

But instead of processing her news about winning the lottery, all he could do was think about how incredibly sexy she looked. Even in ragged jeans and slouchy yellow sweatshirt, with her blond hair bound haphazardly atop her head in something vaguely resembling a ponytail. If you disregarded all those straggly pieces framing her face. Although even those straggly pieces were awfully sexy. Made a man want to lift a hand and skim it oh-so-slowly over her—

"I know it's hard to believe," she said, interrupting what had promised to be a damned nice fantasy. She paced restlessly from one side of his living room to the other, her sock-clad feet silent on the expansive, expensive Aubusson.

"But it's true. It's true!" she cried again, pivoting around to smile at him. "I won the lottery, Marcus! I'm rich! I'm rich! I'm rich!"

"You'll *be* rich," he reminded her. "On Monday."

"Right," she agreed, sobering. Some. For a second or two.

Then she started bouncing up and down on the balls of her feet, her smile dazzling. She paced to the other side of the room, perched herself on the edge of an exquisite Chippendale chair for a nanosecond, then shot up and started pacing again.

"You have to help me, Marcus," she told him as she passed by him quickly enough to create a breeze.

"I'll help you," he promised. "First by fixing you a double Stoli, straight up. I think you could use it."

She spun around with enough force to send a less grounded individual spinning right out of the room. "No, no, no, no, no. Not necessary," she told him. "I'm intoxicated enough as it is."

He feigned disappointment. "What? You started happy hour without me? That's not like you, Dinah."

She smiled at his mention of their usual Friday evening ritual. Dinah worked at home as a freelance writer, so she invariably heard Marcus return home from his architectural firm every day. Over the past three months, it had become their custom to spend every Friday after work enjoying cocktails and conversation together. It had become even more customary for the two of them to have dinner together at one or the other's apartment a couple of times a week.

They'd struck up a nice friendship within days of her moving into the building. It was just too damned bad she wasn't interested in him romantically. But she'd never shown any sign that she returned his very profound interest in her, so he hadn't pressed the issue. Not that he could understand for a minute *why* she wouldn't be interested in him. He'd never had that problem with women before. Ah, well. It wasn't his to question why. But it *was* his to keep his fantasies about Dinah to himself.

"You have to help me, Marcus," she said again, bringing his attention back to the matter at hand. Pretty much. He did still kind of wonder what she had on under that sweatshirt.

"I'll be glad to," he told her. "What do you want me to do? Water your plants while you're gone?"

She started bouncing up and down again. "No, I want you to come with me," she said, her brown eyes wide with excitement.

The drink he'd been lifting to his mouth stopped just short of completing the action. "Come with you?" he echoed. "Why?"

"Because I'm going to need another driver."

"What are you talking about?" Marcus asked. "You're planning to drive to Georgia? By Monday?"

"If we take turns at the wheel, we can drive straight through. We won't have to stop except for food and restrooms."

He eyed her curiously for a moment. "Why would *we* want to do that, when *you* can hop on a plane and be there within hours?"

Her expression went vaguely horrified. "A *plane?*" she repeated, voicing the word as if it were something unspeakably vile. "I can't get on a plane. No way."

He rolled his eyes. "Oh, no. Don't. Dinah. Don't tell me you're one of those people who's afraid of flying."

She made a mild face at him. "Well, of *course* I'm not afraid of flying. Just how flaky do you think I am?"

He sighed in relief. "Good. So what's the problem?"

"It's because of the curse," she told him.

Marcus was afraid to ask. Nevertheless, "The curse?" he repeated cautiously.

Dinah nodded. "Yeah. The curse. The gypsy curse."

# Two

It had taken her forty-five minutes to convince him to accompany her to Georgia, two hours for them to pack and shower and tie up loose ends and plot their driving strategy, twenty minutes to argue over whose car they would take, and thirty minutes to get out of San Francisco.

Now as they sped east, with San Francisco Bay shimmering beneath them like smooth black satin, Dinah felt herself relaxing for the first time since the call to the Georgia Lottery.

Until Marcus said, "Okay, you promised if I came with you, you'd tell me about this gypsy curse."

Oh, yeah. That. Funny how blackmail had a bad habit of backfiring on a person.

She sighed heavily. "Well, it's sort of complicated."

He chuckled wryly. "Yeah, I bet. Family curses sorta tend to be that way."

She nodded. "True." But she said nothing more, hoping he might take the hint and let it go.

No such luck.

"Dinah?"

"Hmm?"

"The curse?"

"Right."

She continued to gaze out the window as she spoke, though, because she didn't want to see Marcus's expression as she explained. People who didn't suffer from family curses just never got the whole family curse thing.

"It dates back to the seventeenth century," she began. "According to the story, one of my more vicious Meade ancestors—not that there were a lot of vicious Meade ancestors," she hastened to clarify. "Most of them were totally passive and decent. In fact, the ones who first came to this country in the 1800s were Quakers who—"

"Dinah?"

"Hmm?"

"The curse?"

"Right." She backpedaled and started again. "This ancestor, apparently obsessed with a beautiful, young gypsy girl, kidnapped her and locked her way up in the tower of his castle. And to get even with him—and to prevent him from committing his nefarious deeds—her family put a curse on him that would also hex all of his ensuing progeny.

"Which I guess is understandable," she qualified, "all things considered. I mean, if someone locked up a member of my family way, way up in a dark, dank, stinky tower and tried to commit nefarious deeds with them, I'd want to do a lot more than put a curse on him. I'd want to wrap both hands around his throat and—"

"Dinah."

"Hmm?"

"The curse."

"Right. Where was I?"

Marcus glanced over at her with narrowed eyes. "The, uh, the curse," he told her.

"Right," she said again. "To make a long story short—"

"Please do."

"—what the curse amounts to," she continued, "is that anytime anybody in my family tries to travel higher than a certain height, something nefarious happens to them. In the case of my vicious ancestor, it was spontaneous combustion."

Marcus swerved into the shoulder a bit, but recovered admirably. "Spontaneous combustion?" he echoed.

Dinah nodded. "Pretty nefarious, huh?"

"You said it."

He glanced over at her again, and the slash of illumination from a bluish-tinted street lamp briefly threw his features into stark contrasts of shadow and light. He had such incredible cheekbones, she noted, not for the first time. And he looked so handsome and dramatic, all dressed in black—black jeans, black sweater, black leather jacket.

Two words, she thought. *Yum. Mee.* And two more words. *Major loss.* To the feminine gender, at any rate. Honestly, it sure was a good thing that she was a level-headed woman. Otherwise, she might very well have fallen in love with him by now. And wouldn't *that* just be about the dumbest thing she'd ever done in her life?

Yeah, good thing she was so levelheaded.

"So how high a height are we talking here?" Marcus asked, stirring her from her musings.

"Well, tower-height, obviously," Dinah replied. "Though the castle was up on a big hill, too, so a bit higher than tower height, I guess. It was the only way the gypsy family could keep my ancestor from committing those nefarious deeds. It's also why so many members of my family live at sea level, and why none of us work in tall buildings. If anyone in my family goes too high up, we pay for it. Big-time."

"How so? Surely someone in your family has tested the curse by now, haven't they? After all, it's been hundreds of years."

"Oh, yes. Several people have tested the curse."

"And?"

"They've all met with nefarious ends."

There was a moment of silence from Marcus, then, "What happened to them?" he asked.

"Oh, gosh, all kinds of things," Dinah said. "For example, there was my Uncle Sebastian, who tried to climb Mount McKinley."

"And what happened to him?"

She shrugged. "We think he was carried off by a California Condor. They never found his body. Except for his one shoe," she clarified.

"His shoe?"

"And his Coors belt buckle."

Marcus said nothing in response to that.

"And then there was my father's cousin, Tilda. She took a job on the 37th floor of a skyscraper once, even though everyone warned her not to."

"And, um, what happened to Tilda? Did she disappear, too?"

"Well, not physically."

Another one of those thoughtful glances from Marcus was followed by his softly muttered, "Um, what does that mean?"

"Well, Tilda's still around," Dinah said. "Pretty much. Physically, anyway."

"Which means?" he asked, clearly with some reluctance.

"Well, she spends a lot of her time these days talking to Czar Nicholas."

"Ah. I see."

"And Oliver Cromwell."

"I got it, Dinah."

"And then there was my great-great grandmother Oneida who—"

"Dinah?"

"Hmm?"

"I got it."

"Oh. Okay."

With a sigh of contentment that she and Marcus were well and truly on their way, Dinah settled back in her seat and gazed out the window at the swiftly passing night.

And she wondered how much longer 'til they got there.


A couple of hours later, Marcus was wondering much the same thing…when he wasn't still marveling at what Dinah had told him earlier. A family curse. Why did this not surprise him? Not that he'd ever considered her to be flaky. Well, not *too* flaky, anyway. Not really. No, he liked to think of Dinah as being… unconventional. Yeah, that was a good word for her. Unconventional and…hot.

Yeah, *hot* was another good word for Dinah Meade. Especially decked out, as she was now, in snug, faded jeans and a cropped red sweater that kept riding up over her torso, every time she twisted in her seat—which was frequently, because she wasn't the kind of person who liked to sit still.

It was even worse when she reached into the backseat for something. And so far on this trip, she'd reached back there for a lot. First for a bottle of water from the cooler, then for a bag of chips from the hamper, then for one of the maps they'd bought when they'd gassed up.

And every time she went over that seat, Marcus nearly drove right off the road, because her denim-clad rump and her creamy naked torso had been right there for the taking, had he a mind to take them—which he did—and the freedom of movement to manage it—which he didn't. But, gee, they'd have to stop eventually, wouldn't they?

In spite of Dinah's cockamamy idea that they'd drive straight through, Marcus couldn't see any harm in stopping briefly at a hotel along the way to get some decent sleep.

Or something.

Yeah, maybe, he thought, this cross-country drive wasn't such a bad idea, after all. So pressing the accelerator just the tiniest bit closer to the floor, he pushed thoughts of business aside, glanced over at his companion and said, "Hey, Dinah. How about reaching back there to get me a bottle of water?"

"Sure thing, Marcus." She unhooked her seatbelt and joked, "Don't wreck," as she knelt on the seat and turned backward to accommodate his request.

Inescapably his attention drifted from the road to the

nicely rounded bottom that was now right at eye level, and at the tantalizing band of flesh that peeked out between her blue jeans and sweater. And he tried really hard to steer his gaze back to the highway. Unfortunately, his eyes were slow to follow his command, because Dinah chose that moment to shift positions, and the sway of her rump was just too tempting to ignore. By the time Marcus did finally remember to pay attention to what he was doing, it was too late.

There, dead center of the highway—ooh, bad choice of words, he thought vaguely—were about a million flashing red-and-blue lights fixed atop roughly a billion emergency response vehicles. In one rapid, crystal clear instant, Marcus accomplished several things. He reminded himself that Dinah wasn't buckled in. He threw his right arm across the back of her legs in a valiant, if totally futile, effort to protect her. He stomped his foot hard on the brake.

And he hoped like hell he could stop in time.

# Three

Then she ceased to think at all, because her back was slamming into the dashboard, the SUV was skittering sideways and the tires were crunching over what sounded very much like death. But, strangely, of all the scary realizations running through Dinah's cognitive system in that moment, one rose way above all the others: *Marcus has his hand on my butt. What the...?*

Then that thought, too, evaporated. Not because Marcus's hand moved, but because the SUV stopped. The SUV stopped, but Dinah's heart kept racing. Which meant, she finally understood, that she was alive.

"Um, Marcus?" she finally asked in a very small voice.

"Yes, Dinah?" His voice, she noted, was remarkably steady.

"What, uh...what exactly just happened?"

"Well, Dinah, we, um...we almost died."

"That's what I thought. Marcus?"

"Yes, Dinah?"

"You can, uh...you can take your hand off my, uh, my, um... You can take your hand off me now."

Only then did he seem to realize where she'd landed, but instead of jerking his hand off of her bottom, which was pretty much what Dinah had figured he would do, Marcus only gazed at her blindly for a moment and continued to keep his hand right where it was.

Which, Dinah decided vaguely, actually wasn't such a bad thing. Especially when he opened his hand more fully over her fanny and curled his fingers more intimately against her, sending a shot of white-hot need rocketing through her entire body.

*Oh, my.*

"Marcus?" she said, her voice trembling. She was stunned by the unmistakable passion and desire that darkened his eyes. But he wasn't supposed to be feeling passionate or full of desire. Not here, in the middle of I-5 South. Not now, when they'd both just been snatched from the jaws of death. Not with her, someone who had two X chromosomes.

Then, suddenly, Dinah understood. They really had just been snatched from the jaws of death. And didn't she recall something from a college Psych 101 class about people becoming more sexually active after a brush with death, because the sex act was so ultimately life-affirming?

Or had she read that in a copy of *True Confessions* magazine? She always got those two confused.

At any rate, that was surely what was at the root of Marcus's reaction now. He'd just narrowly escaped death. At this point, he'd probably be turned on by anyone who was processing oxygen. And Dinah was most definitely doing that, if her still ragged breathing was any indication.

"Are you okay?" he asked, scattering her jumbled thoughts.

She nodded, unable to say a word, uncertain what to say, even if she could speak.

He inhaled a deep breath and closed his eyes tightly, and Dinah took advantage of his preoccupation to scramble back into her seat. After that, anything else they might have said—or done—was prevented by the arrival of a police officer, tapping at the driver's side window.

With one last fortifying breath, Marcus rolled down the window and pasted on a phony smile. "Is there a problem, officer?" he asked very politely.

She studied her watch and thought about her five million dollars. And she wondered what else on this trip could go wrong.

Shortly after daybreak Saturday morning, Marcus awoke in the passenger seat from a nap that had been anything but restful, just in time to see a sign that read, "You are now leaving Denby, Arizona. Have a nice day."

He snagged the map from the pocket in the door beside him and scanned it until he found Denby, his gaze traveling a lot farther west than he'd hoped it would. He shook his head ruefully. They weren't making good time at all. At this rate, Dinah would be lucky to claim a coat check ticket, if not a lottery jackpot. They were going to have to do something to pick up the speed.

"You want to change drivers again?" he asked as he

launched himself into a full-body stretch. Or at least as much of a full-body stretch as the cramped vehicle would allow. He braced his forearms against the ceiling and extended his legs forward as far as he could, then pushed hard. Oh, boy, that felt good.

Dinah seemed to be feeling pretty good herself, because when she glanced over at him, her eyes went wide with...something. Something warm. Something wild. Something that looked very much like... appreciation? Well, well, well. Maybe he'd finally discovered the secret to attracting her attention. Take her on a road trip, drive all night and almost get her killed, then, when exhaustion started to kick in, boom, she was his.

Okay, so maybe she wasn't quite his. Not yet, anyway. She was, clearly, exhausted. Faint purple crescents smudged her eyes, and she looked sort of limp all over. Although she, too, had napped briefly during the night, he knew she hadn't actually slept. Despite the fact that they were making lousy time, they really were going to have to stop somewhere before long to get some proper sleep.

Or something.

"Maybe when we stop for breakfast we can switch," she said, returning her attention to the road ahead, and Marcus's attention to the matter at hand.

He gazed through the windshield, too, and saw a long, black ribbon of highway bisecting two vast plains of colorless nothingness. "Where?" he asked. "Looks like we're out in the middle of nowhere."

"There was nothing in the last town, but the next one is only about a half hour away. We can find something there."

Marcus wondered if he should introduce into the

conversation what was no doubt on both their minds, or let them both go on being deluded for a while longer. Ultimately, though, he decided, *What the hell,* and said, "You realize, of course, that we're making remarkably bad time."

Dinah said nothing, only kept her gaze fixed on the road.

"Dinah?" he prodded.

She expelled a restless sound. "We can make it up. We still have plenty of time."

"We're going to have to stop at hotel tonight to get some decent sleep."

She shook her head. "That won't be necessary."

"Dinah…"

"We'll make it."

"I'm just thinking it might be better if we—"

"We'll make it, Marcus. We'll make it."

Hoo-kay, he thought, relenting. Score one for delusion. And speaking of delusions…

"So tell me some more about this family curse," he said suddenly. Maybe, if nothing else, he could get Dinah to admit that the family curse thing was a lot of hooey.

"What about it?" she asked.

"You don't honestly buy into all that hoodoo. Do you? I mean, we could catch a plane at the next big city, and—"

"No." Her reply was swift and adamant.

"But this is a new millennium," he reminded her. "And surely there's some kind of statute of limitations on curses."

"Well, I don't know about a statute of limitations," she conceded, "but, according to family legend, there *is* one way to break the curse."

Well, that certainly helped, Marcus thought. "And that would be?"

She hesitated a moment. "Supposedly, any Meade who finds true love with someone—really, truly, wonderfully true love—then that's supposed to break the curse for that particular Meade."

"True love?" Marcus echoed.

"True love," Dinah confirmed.

"Well, you know, all things considered, that's not such a bad way to break a curse."

"Oh, sure. Easy for you to say. But where am I supposed to find true love in this day and age?" she demanded. "Nobody finds true love anymore."

Oh, now *that* was a matter of opinion, Marcus thought. He opened his mouth to say just that when Dinah cut him off.

"All of the good ones are taken," she told him. "Or else all of the good ones are gay."

Marcus narrowed his eyes at her. "You really think so?"

"I know so."

Well, that didn't sound very promising. How could Dinah not think he was one of the good ones? 'Cause he sure wasn't taken. He opened his mouth to say just that when the SUV cut him off.

Because it skittered wildly, jolting him back to awareness. And the first thing he became aware of was that Dinah was having some major difficulty maneuvering the big SUV. The second thing he became aware of was that it was because they had a flat tire.

He gritted his teeth and held on tight as she downshifted, slowed and gradually pulled the vehicle to the side of the road. And he admired the coolness with which she handled everything.

That coolness, however, turned into frozenness the moment the truck came to a complete halt. Because all she did was sit stock-still, staring straight ahead, her knuckles white as she gripped the wheel with both hands.

"Dinah?" he asked softly. "You okay?"

No response from the driver, save some erratic breathing.

"Dinah?" Marcus tried again.

Nothing.

He reached across the seat and carefully pried her fingers free, then wove them with his own, only to find that they were as rigid and cold as an icicle.

"Dinah," he tried again. "It's okay. We're okay. We'll just have to change the tire, that's all."

Finally, finally, she seemed to realize what had happened. But when she glanced over at Marcus, her eyes were huge and shiny with tears. "We're not going to make it, are we?" she said. "I might as well just kiss that five million bucks goodbye."

# Four

Of course, finding a gas station open so early on a Saturday in such a small, by-the-way town, and replacing Marcus's spare tire with a new one helped, too.

With their stomachs full, their spirits lifted and their mental attitudes improved, Dinah and Marcus generated some exceedingly good karma. For the rest of the weekend, they made excellent time, with nary an overturned semi, flat tire or traffic jam in sight. By midnight Sunday, they had crossed into Mississippi and were feeling pretty celebratory.

They were also feeling pretty sleepy.

"We need to stop for a while, Dinah," Marcus said from the driver's side. "We need to find a hotel, if just for a few hours. I'm beat."

*Beat* didn't even begin to cover how she was feeling herself. More than forty-eight hours had passed since she'd showered or changed her clothes, and she knew she must look as ragged as she felt. In spite of that, she offered halfheartedly, "I'll take over the driving for a bit."

He shook his head. "You're no better rested than I am."

"Sure I am," she countered wearily. "I slept for a while this afternoon."

He expelled an incredulous sound. "Yeah, right."

"Okay," she conceded, "maybe I didn't actually sleep, per se, but I did nap for a while."

"Uh-huh."

"Okay, so maybe it wasn't napping so much as it was dozing. I did doze. Some."

"Mmm-hmm."

"Well, maybe it wasn't a lot of dozing, but I did have a dream," she told him.

"Oh, really?" he asked dubiously. "About what?"

Actually, Dinah recalled now, it had been a dream about Marcus. And in that dream, Marcus had been doing things with her, *to* her, that she would just as soon not describe to him in detail right now. Or ever. Her face flamed when she remembered some of the more explicit, more erotic, highlights.

Oh, boy, was she glad she wasn't the kind of woman to fall in love easily. Because if she was, after that dream... Well. Between the passion she'd experienced for him in that dream, and the easy camaraderie she shared with him in real life, Dinah would definitely be over the moon by now where her feelings for Marcus were concerned.

"The dream was about, uh...a, um..." She scrambled for some kind of explanation and blurted out the first thing that popped into her head. "It was about a powerful locomotive speeding through a dark tunnel."

Gee, now why would that be the first thing that popped into her head? Dinah wondered. Then she recalled something else from her Psych 101 class—or *True Confessions* magazine. Something about how a powerful locomotive speeding through a dark tunnel was symbolic of something... Symbolic of...of...of...

Uh-oh.

"A powerful locomotive speeding through a dark tunnel, huh?" Marcus echoed with a chuckle. "Interesting dream."

*Boy, you don't know the half of it.*

But all Dinah could manage in response was, "Um, yeah. It was. Interesting, I mean."

Marcus chuckled some more. "We definitely need to stop and get some sleep. We're starting to get punchy."

Dinah sighed, relenting. He was right. It would be dangerous for them to operate any kind of heavy machinery in their current mental states. Then again, she pondered further, did she really want to check into a motel with Marcus in her *own* current mental state?

Then again, she pondered further still, what difference did it make? He wasn't going to make a pass at *her.* And he'd rebuff any pass she might make at him. Not that she had any intention of making a pass at Marcus.

*In your dreams, Dinah.*

Well, okay, maybe there. But only there.

"I guess you're right," she finally surrendered. She noted the next mile marker she saw, then pulled out the map and flicked on the overhead light. "We should be hitting a town called Garvey in about forty-five minutes. It looks big enough to have at least one decent motel. Maybe if we just check in for a few hours, we won't lose too much time. We should still make Georgia by late afternoon with no problem."

*I hope.*

They remained silent after that, both of them probably too tired to do much more than concentrate on staying conscious long enough to cover the next forty miles. Dinah, however, didn't have to concentrate as hard as Marcus did over there in the driver's seat, and, inescapably, her mind wandered back to the dream she'd enjoyed that afternoon. Boy, had she enjoyed it. Yepper. Probably way more than she should have.

Her mind then wandered back further still to their near miss on the highway two nights before, when she'd landed in Marcus's capable hands. Or rather in his capable hand. Quite literally, in fact. Which, now that she thought about it, might be what had sparked that odd dream. Because in her dream, he'd had his hand on a lot more than her—

But that wasn't really important, she told herself. What was important was that she needed sleep. Because exhaustion could be the only explanation for why she was thinking the things she was thinking, and feeling the things she was feeling. Exhaustion. Nothing more.

*Yeah, that's the ticket.*

Normally, it would have caused Dinah some concern to be alone with a man in a hotel room, wearing nothing but a little white towel. But Marcus was still in the shower, and she was having an awful lot of trouble finding the underwear she was sure she'd packed in her duffel bag. And the man in question was Marcus, who wouldn't even notice her little white towel because it was wrapped around—sort of—a body that just didn't do anything for him.

Would that she could say the same about the little white towel wrapped around—sort of—his body when he stepped out of the bathroom then, a body that did, oh...a lot for her.

They'd both collapsed onto separate beds immediately upon entering the room three hours ago and now felt rested enough to continue with their grand adventure. But they'd both wanted—nay, *needed*—showers before continuing, even if it did cost them precious time. They could make it to Georgia by this afternoon, Dinah promised herself. They could.

They could.

Now, as Marcus stepped out of the bathroom, surrounded by billows of steam and that little scrap of terry cloth, Dinah couldn't quite quell the spiral of wanting—and something else, too, something less distinct, but infinitely more troubling—that wound tighter inside her.

His dark hair was wet, slicked straight back from his face, and his cheeks were ruddy from his recent shave. Dark hair covered the ropes of muscle and sinew on his chest, swirling down over a flat torso to disappear into the towel. She watched as he dragged a comb through his hair, biting back a wistful sigh at the way his biceps and triceps, and oh, my goodness, those *abs,* danced to an erotic tune playing in her head.

And she couldn't halt the blush that crept into her face when his gaze met hers in the mirror, and he caught her ogling him so blatantly. Immediately, he spun around to face her, his own cheeks ruddy, his expression bordering on stunned.

Oh, yeah, she'd bet he was stunned. Nothing like

having a woman panting after you when all you felt for her was a fond and friendly affection.

"Dinah?" he asked, his voice low and husky and very aroused.

Honestly, if she hadn't known better, Dinah would have sworn the man was completely turned on. But, of course, she knew better. There was no way Marcus could be turned on by her.

Could he?

Before she could ponder that particular quandary, he pitched the comb onto the sink and made his way slowly, deliberately, and oh-so-sexily, across the room. He said nothing as he approached, only held her gaze steadily with his own. And when he dropped down to sit on the bed beside her, something made her clutch her towel more resolutely to her chest.

"You, uh…you got something on your mind?" he asked softly. "Something maybe I should know?" Then, to her surprise, he lifted a hand and nudged a strand of hair near her face back behind her ear.

"Um, no," she lied. "Not really."

He nodded slowly, withdrawing his hand, but only to skim the pad of his thumb gingerly along her jaw line. "Funny," he murmured. "'Cause you really look like you have something on your mind that I should know about."

Dinah swallowed hard, and when she did, Marcus dropped his gaze, then his hand, to her throat, curving his fingers intimately over her nape. The heat that curled through her was keen and piercing and very demanding.

"No," she said again, her voice coming out thready and embarrassingly squeaky. "It's nothing."

"C'mon," he cajoled, stroking his thumb along the

column of her throat with a maddening gentleness. "You can tell me."

Dinah eyed him levelly, her thoughts, assumptions and doubts all colliding at once in her brain. "What are you doing?" she asked quietly, thinking it a very good question.

His lips turned up in a very seductive smile. "What? You can't tell? Maybe I should work a little harder."

*Oh, my.*

"Hmm?" he said, his mouth hovering a scant inch from hers.

"But...but, Marcus..." she tried again.

"Yes, Dinah?"

"But...but..."

"But what?" he asked, his voice a little less seductive now.

"But I thought...I thought..."

"You thought *what?*" he asked.

"I...I thought you... I thought you were...were..."

"You thought I was *what?*"

"Marcus, I thought you were...gay?"

Gay? *Gay?*

Well, this was news to Marcus. "Gay?" he echoed. "Gay? How the hell could you think I was *gay?*"

She plucked nervously at the blanket beneath her. "Well," she said quietly, "you *are* a single man living in San Francisco."

He studied her blankly for a moment, telling himself that couldn't possibly be the extent of her assumption. But when she said nothing more, he replied, "Um, yeah. As are thousands of other heterosexual men. What else made you think I'm gay?"

"Well," she tried again, "you do dress very nicely."

He continued to eye her intently. "And?"

"And you always smell so nice," she pointed out.

"And?"

"You're an *excellent* dancer."

He pinched the bridge of his nose. "Dinah, how many more pieces of this stereotype puzzle are we going to add?"

"You have the soundtrack for West Side Story,'" she added.

"It has that kickass Leonard Bernstein score," he replied. He pointed a finger at her and stated, quite adamantly, "Hey, that's the most macho show that ever hit Broadway."

"But it *is* a musical," she reminded him.

He sighed heavily.

"Well, it *is*."

Marcus muttered an impatient sound. "What else?" he asked wearily. "Might as well just get all this out in the open now."

"Well, you used the word 'fussy' once."

He gaped at her. "I have *never* used the word 'fussy.'"

She nodded. Vehemently. "Oh, yes, you did, too."

"When?"

"That first day I met you in the lobby, when we were talking about the window treatments."

Marcus searched his brain, trying very hard to recall the episode. Not surprisingly, however, he came up completely blank. "Nope. Sorry. Didn't happen. You must have misunderstood."

Boy, was that an understatement.

"Well, anyway, you're much too good to be true," Dinah finally concluded. "Certainly much too good to be heterosexual."

Marcus gazed at her for a long, silent moment, wondering just how to proceed. Suddenly, it all made sense, why she'd never returned his interest. And he realized then that he should have tried just a tad bit harder to illustrate that interest. Especially since he was beginning to understand that what he felt for Dinah was a lot more than just *interest*. He only hoped it wasn't too late.

"Dinah," he finally said softly. "Dearest. I assure you, I am not homosexual."

"Oh, please, Marcus, you don't have to pretend with me. I'm a very open-minded person. In fact—"

She never got to finish what she was going to say, because Marcus took it upon himself to prove his assertion to her the only way he knew how.

He kissed her. Soundly. Towels be damned.

# Five

Well, actually, she didn't notice too much after that.

Because Marcus deepened the kiss, covering her mouth with his, and tasted her passionately, intimately, thoroughly. He skimmed his fingers lightly along her jaw, brushed his bent knuckles down the side of her neck, dipped his forefinger into the elegant hollow at the base of her throat.

Little by little, Dinah was drawn under his spell, and it felt so good to finally be doing something she had wanted to do for a very long while. All this time she'd been thinking Marcus couldn't be interested in her, not in the way she was interested in him. All this time she'd thought it would be pointless to pursue anything with him. All this time she'd been so certain he would never, could never, return her feelings for him.

All this time she'd been wrong. Oh, boy, had she been wrong. And now... Well now just about anything seemed possible. And now all those feelings she'd been feeling for him were starting to make sense and ceasing to seem pointless.

Heat bubbled up inside her as she lifted a hand to his hair, threading her fingers through the damp, silky tresses. Her touch must have stirred something more insistent in him because he looped his arm fiercely around her waist and pulled her closer still. Two brief scraps of fabric were all that came between them then. There was nothing more than that to prevent them from doing what they both so obviously wanted to do. Nothing except those two brief scraps of fabric, and—

Five million dollars.

"Stop!" she cried, jerking away from him. "We don't have time for this right now!"

Marcus grinned devilishly, reaching for her again. With one swift, deft maneuver, he hauled her back into his arms. "Oh, Dinah. There's *always* time for this."

He burrowed his head against her neck and dragged his open mouth along her throat, his breath hot and damp and tantalizing against her skin. And Dinah had to admit then that maybe he might have a point....

She doubled both fists loosely against his chest and pushed him back. But not too far. "Is it worth sacrificing five million dollars?" she asked pointedly.

He thought about that for a moment. "Yeah, actually. As a matter of fact, I think it is."

She gaped at him. Well, when he put it like *that*.... "Wow," she whispered reverently. He must be really, really good.

His grin turned roguish. "Oh, baby, 'wow' doesn't even begin to describe what we're about to do."

She wanted so badly to give in to her desires and spend the rest of the night—hey, the rest of the week—

right there in that hotel room, exploring things with Marcus she had only dreamed about enjoying before. And she came very, very close to doing so. But even without the five million dollars waiting for her in Georgia, things with Marcus were happening much too fast.

In a way, she'd just met him. All this time she'd been thinking he was someone else. It was going to take a while before she could adjust to viewing him in this new, heterosexual light.

At least, you know, a couple of hours.

"Marcus, we can't do this right now."

He opened his mouth to object, but Dinah cut him off.

"There's more than my lottery jackpot to consider here. There's...there's...um..."

"Yes?" he prodded, dipping his head to nuzzle the sensitive place where her neck joined her shoulder. Oh, that was very, very nice. "There's...what?" he asked.

He pulled her close again, opening his hand over her back, covering her mouth with his. Oh, that was so good. So right. So very, very... *Oh*.

Dinah curled her fingers over his naked shoulders, his skin feeling like hot satin beneath her fingertips. Then she splayed her other hand open over his heart, finding comfort in the discovery that his pulse was racing as erratically as her own.

"We can't," she said again, albeit reluctantly. "Marcus, please. We can't. Not now. Not...yet."

It was that final word that made Marcus surrender to her insistence. Not that he didn't think he could make her change her mind if given another, oh, three or four seconds. But Dinah was right. Even without the money waiting for her at the end of their journey, this wasn't a good idea. Not yet.

He cared for Dinah in ways that he'd never cared for another woman. She was funny and smart and cute, and he felt more comfortable around her than he did anyone else he knew. Hell, he might as well just admit it to himself—he was halfway in love with her. Maybe even all the way in love with her. He could wait a little longer for her to get used to the idea of the two of them together.

But not *too* much longer.

*Not yet,* she'd told him. He could do a lot with *not yet.* In twelve hours, if all went well, they ought to be rolling into Atlanta. They had until the lottery head-quarters closed at five-thirty to claim her prize. And once that was done, he imagined she was going to feel like celebrating. Celebrating her wealth. Celebrating her financial security. Celebrating the success of her journey. Celebrating this newfound...whatever it was... between them.

And if there was one thing Marcus Harrod was very good at, it was celebrating. Especially with Dinah Meade.

*Not yet,* he mused again. He guessed he'd just have to settle for that. For now.


They were just ten miles shy of the Georgia border when they stopped for gas. Which was just as well, Dinah thought as they rolled to a stop at one of the pumps and Marcus turned off the engine. She had to use the ladies' room, anyway. Plus, she'd really been craving an Almond Joy for the past hundred miles.

The mini-mart was hopping, she noted as she jumped down from the SUV. She and Marcus were going to have a bit of a wait to pay for their gas. Good thing it was still early afternoon. Atlanta was no more than two hours away, which gave them a good two-hour cushion. They had plenty of time to claim her jackpot.

She fished her wallet out of her purse and checked the contents, only to discover—surprise, surprise—that the cash compartment was empty. Boy, that five million bucks couldn't come fast enough. Dinah could almost feel the check in her hands—the smooth, cool paper, all those wonderful zeroes.... Oh, this was going to be *great*. The first thing she would do was treat Marcus to a wildly expensive dinner. And after that...

She couldn't wait to find out if she was right.

Especially since part of what she suspected was going to happen involved a lot more than a physical union. She was reasonably certain that there would be quite an emotional union happening, too. At least, there would be on her part. Because now that she knew Marcus did, in fact, go for estrogen-producing individuals, she could stop denying the fact that she'd been halfway in love with the guy for months. And then, maybe, if all went well, she could stop denying the fact that she'd been halfway in love with him for months, and admit that she was completely in love with him for all time. And then maybe, just maybe, he might come to return her feelings.

"Hey, Marcus," she said, nudging aside her thoughts for the moment. "Could you loan me a couple of bucks?" She smiled her most dazzling smile. "You know I'm good for it."

He smiled back. "Boy, you kiss a woman once, and what happens? She wants to borrow money from you."

Dinah blushed. "Um, I thought we agreed not to talk about that until after I've claimed my prize and we can do it without distraction."

His smile turned lascivious. "Yeah, and I'm really looking forward to doing it without distraction, too."

"Marcus…"

He chuckled as he withdrew his wallet from the back pocket of his blue jeans and pitched it to her. "Take what you need. I know where you live."

"Thanks," she told him, catching it capably in both hands. "I'll pay for the gas while I'm inside."

"I'll meet you in there," he offered. "I want to pick up a couple of things, too."

Ten minutes later, Dinah ran into him in the candy bar aisle, filling his hands with as many Hershey bars as he could carry. At her laughter, he glanced up, shrugging guiltily.

"Hey, I figure we'll be celebrating in a little while," he said in his defense. "I want to be prepared."

"I've never seen a man go after chocolate the way you do," she replied. "I knew you were too good to be heterosexual."

"Hey, hey, *hey*," he said indignantly. "I thought we settled that little misconception earlier."

"Yeah, well, I'm not quite convinced yet."

"Guess I have my work cut out for me, proving it to you."

"Guess you do."

She nudged his shoulder with hers, then he nudged her back with his, and they continued nudging each other and laughing as they paid for their purchases. Then, as Dinah unwrapped her Almond Joy, Marcus held the door open for her, and she preceded him through it. But she straggled behind, and he quickly took the lead.

She was so busy with her task, in fact, that she didn't

pay attention to where she was going. Not until she bumped into Marcus's back.

When she glanced up to find out why he'd stopped, she saw him gaping at something in the distance. And when she trailed her gaze after his, she understood what it was that had made him stop and gape. Except that stopping and gaping didn't quite cover Dinah's own reaction to the scene. No, this called for considerably more than stopping and gaping.

"Oh, my God, Marcus!" she yelled at the top of her lungs. "Somebody stole the car!"

# Six

Ignition. Dammit. He'd left the keys in the ignition. With all the exhaustion, and all the excitement of being so close to Georgia, and all the relief at surviving the trip, and all the distraction that came with replaying in his head those mind-scrambling, libido-twisting, emotion-tangling kisses he'd shared with Dinah, Marcus just hadn't been thinking. And now his truck was gone.

Then another, much worse, thought struck him.

"Dinah," he said. Reining in his panic, he turned and placed his hands on her shoulders. "The lottery ticket," he added. "Dinah, where's the lottery ticket?"

For one terrifying moment, he thought she was going to tell him that it had gone the way of the stolen SUV. Then she slapped a hand against the purse hanging at her side and expelled a gasp of relief.

"Here," she said. "It's here in my wallet."

"Oh, thank God."

Their mutual relief was short-lived, however.

"Marcus," she said softly, "what are we going to do? Somebody stole the car."

He inhaled a deep breath and expelled it slowly. "First, we're going to call the police."

"But—"

"Then we'll find a way to get to Atlanta."

"But—"

"We still have plenty of time, Dinah."

"We have less than four hours, Marcus."

"Which is plenty of time," he insisted.

She closed her eyes tightly for a moment, but the gesture wasn't enough to stop the eruption of two fat tears that squeezed through, tumbling down her cheeks in twin streams.

"Oh, Dinah," he said, gathering her into his arms. "It'll be okay, I promise. We haven't come all this way just to be foiled at the last minute. We'll make it."

She burrowed her head into his chest and looped her arms around his waist. "We were so close," she mumbled against his sweater. "So close."

"We're still close," he assured her. "We're less than a hundred miles from Atlanta. And hell, if we have to run that last hundred miles, we will."

"We're not going to make it," she said again.

"Oh, yes, we are, too," he immediately countered. "We'll make it by five-thirty. I promise you, Dinah. I promise you."

The state troopers were completely sympathetic to their plight, and, once they understood the situation, hurried through their report as quickly as they could. They even offered Dinah and Marcus a ride, something that went a long way toward restoring her faith in humanity.

Until the troopers pulled their car into the grassy median just before reaching the state line and told them to get out.

"What?" Dinah asked, outraged. But she got out of the car as instructed. She always did buckle to authority. Even when five million dollars was at stake. Dammit.

"Sorry, ma'am," the trooper told her through the driver's side window. "But we can't take the car across the state line."

Dinah narrowed her eyes at the Alabama trooper, her thoughts racing. They'd finally made it to within mere feet of Georgia, but Atlanta was still a good seventy-five miles away. And they only had two hours left until the deadline.

"But we still have to get to Atlanta," she objected.

The trooper shrugged ruefully. "Not our jurisdiction."

She thought for a moment. "Are you telling me that if you were chasing some evil law-breaker, you wouldn't follow him into the next state because it would be out of your jurisdiction?"

"Well, that would depend on the circumstances," he conceded.

She thought for a moment more. "So, like, if I slapped you really hard right now and started running, then you'd—"

"Dinah."

The admonition came not from the trooper, but from Marcus. When she turned to look at him, he had narrowed his own gaze, and set his jaw rather forcefully. "Don't. Even. Think about it," he told her.

She blew out an impatient breath. "I'm just exploring my options, that's all."

The trooper, thankfully, didn't seem offended. In fact, he smiled. "I know you're in a tight fix," he said. "But I called in a little help from one of my Georgia colleagues. It's his day off, but he's agreed to lend a hand."

No sooner were the words out of the trooper's mouth than Dinah registered the sound of a siren. It was quickly punctuated by the arrival of a Georgia state trooper's car, with trooper at the wheel, which pulled to a stop in the median no more than thirty feet away.

"This fella here'll get you where you need to go," the Alabama trooper told her. "And if I know him—which, of course, I do—he'll get you there with time to spare." He lifted a finger to the brim of his Smokey-the-Bear hat. "Y'all have a nice day," he concluded.

Dinah wanted to hug the guy, but she was afraid there might be some kind of civic ordinance against it. So she settled for saying, "Be on the lookout for a big, fat check made out to the Policeman's Ball."

He chuckled. "Well, now, we don't really have a Policeman's Ball. But if you want to contribute something to the Children's Athletic Fund, we'd be much obliged."

"Consider it done," she told him. She turned to the Georgia trooper who had left his car in Georgia and joined them in Alabama. "And if you can get me to Atlanta by five-thirty, I'll do the same for the great state of Georgia."

The other trooper smiled. "Your chariot awaits."

Dinah stretched out on the big king-size bed in her room at the Four Seasons Hotel Atlanta and expelled a very long, very contented sigh. Never in her life had she enjoyed such sumptuous surroundings. Whoever said money couldn't buy happiness simply did not know where to shop.

But Dinah sure did. In fact, she and Marcus had spent the better part of the evening—after their wildly expensive dinner—shopping to replenish their stolen supplies. Of course, seeing as how she was worth millions of dollars more now than she'd been a few hours earlier, those supplies were infinitely nicer than the ones that had accompanied them from San Francisco. For instance, Dinah had never realized just how soft and wonderful butter-yellow silk pajamas could feel against a person's recently bubble-bathed skin.

Of course, not so deep down, she knew it wasn't the money that had brought her the happiness she felt right now. No, it was the sight of Marcus, in his own silk pajamas—sapphire-blue in his case, and he only wore the bottoms—that caused pleasure to curl through her. And it was the knowledge that she loved him so—and that he loved her in return—that inspired all the joy, all the bliss, all the rapture. It was love that brought happiness, not money.

Though she'd be a fool if she didn't admit that the money was pretty swell, too.

"Thank you," Marcus said into the telephone receiver he had cradled between his ear and—deliciously naked—shoulder. "We appreciate it. Yes, we'll be there to pick it up tomorrow afternoon."

The Alabama troopers had found his SUV abandoned a few miles from the service station, the victim, apparently, of a trio of teenagers out to commit their first crime. They'd quickly reconsidered and dumped the vehicle, completely intact, by the side of the road. It was yet another example of Dinah's exceedingly good fortune.

"Finally," she said as Marcus settled the phone into the receiver. "Now you can call room service." She scooped up the piece of paper lying beside her on the bed. "Here. I've very conveniently made you a list."

Marcus grinned as he took it from her and scanned it. "Gee, do you think a magnum of Perrier-Jouet champagne will be enough?"

"It's a start," she told him.

"I thought so, too."

"But I think we should go for the two-pound box of Godiva," he told her. "One pound isn't enough for a celebration like this."

"Mmm," she agreed. "I guess you're right."

He made the required call, then joined her on the bed, stretching out alongside her, pulling her close. He was warm and rosy from his recent shower, redolent of the spicy scents of soap and man. She couldn't resist snuggling against him, didn't bother to quell the purr of satisfaction that wandered up from deep inside her. Oh, boy, was life good.

"So, Dinah," Marcus said softly as he nuzzled the side of her throat. "What are you going to do with all that money?"

She curled her arms around his neck and pulled him close. "Pursue a dream," she told him without hesitation.

"Would it, by any chance, be that dream you had in the car yesterday?" he asked hopefully. "The one with the speeding locomotive rushing through a dark tunnel?"

She laughed. "Well, maybe eventually," she admitted. "But the one I'm talking about is the one I've se-creted away in my heart for a long time now."

He pulled away a little, just enough so that he could gaze down into her face, his blue eyes dreamy and happy. "Is it one I know about?"

She shook her head, but smiled. "It's one I've never told anyone about, because it seemed so impossible to make come true. Until now."

"But now that you know I'm heterosexual, you're going to go after it?" he asked, even more hopefully than before.

She hesitated only a moment before revealing what she'd never revealed to anyone. And somehow, having Marcus be the first was very appropriate. "I want to write the Great American Novel," she told him. "I've never been able to find the time to do it before, but now I can. And that's what I'm going to do. Besides," she hurried on when she saw his smile of approval, "there's more than my discovery of your sexuality that's making me go after you."

"Oh?" he asked, more hopefully than ever.

She nodded. "There's the small matter of me being crazy in love with you."

His smile then went absolutely incandescent. "Gee, that's going to wreak havoc with the ol' Meade curse, isn't it?"

She chuckled low. "Why do you think I insisted on having dinner at the Sun Dial Restaurant, hmm?"

"Seventy-two stories above the city?" he asked mildly. "That did sort of surprise me, when you sug-gested it."

"Did it?"

"Well, no, not really. Because by then, I knew you'd found true love and therefore broken the curse."

ELIZABETH BEVARLY                                     251

This time Dinah was the one to smile. "How did you know that?" she asked.

He curled his fingers around her nape and dipped his forehead to hers. "I know because I feel it, too," he said softly. "I love you, Dinah. Truly."

"And I love you, Marcus. Truly."

For a moment, neither of them said a word, only lay side by side, cuddling, snuggling and feeling really, really happy.

Then, very softly, Marcus said, "Dinah, you need to remember something very important about people who get whatever they want in life."

She sighed with *much* contentment. "What's that?"

He pressed a kiss to her neck, her jaw, her cheek, her mouth, then pulled back to gaze down into her face again. He really was incredibly handsome, she thought. Sexy. Sweet. Funny. Heterosexual. Would her good luck never end?

"Usually," he told her, brushing his lips lightly over hers, "they live happily ever after."

Dinah grinned happily as she sank back into the lush pillows behind her, bringing Marcus down for the ride. "Oh, my," she said softly as she threaded her fingers through his hair. "Then I guess that's exactly what will happen to us."

* * * * *

# PASSION

Harlequin® *Desire*

## COMING NEXT MONTH
### AVAILABLE APRIL 10, 2012

**#2149 FEELING THE HEAT**
*The Westmorelands*
**Brenda Jackson**
Dr. Micah Westmoreland knows Kalina Daniels hasn't forgiven him. But he can't ignore the heat that still burns between them....

**#2150 ON THE VERGE OF I DO**
*Dynasties: The Kincaids*
**Heidi Betts**

**#2151 HONORABLE INTENTIONS**
*Billionaires and Babies*
**Catherine Mann**

**#2152 WHAT LIES BENEATH**
**Andrea Laurence**

**#2153 UNFINISHED BUSINESS**
**Cat Schield**

**#2154 A BREATHLESS BRIDE**
*The Pearl House*
**Fiona Brand**

# REQUEST YOUR FREE BOOKS!
## 2 FREE NOVELS PLUS 2 FREE GIFTS!

### ALWAYS POWERFUL, PASSIONATE AND PROVOCATIVE

**YES!** Please send me 2 FREE Harlequin Desire® novels and my 2 FREE gifts (gifts are worth about $10). After receiving them, if I don't wish to receive any more books, I can return the shipping statement marked "cancel." If I don't cancel, I will receive 6 brand-new novels every month and be billed just $4.30 per book in the U.S. or $4.99 per book in Canada. That's a saving of at least 14% off the cover price! It's quite a bargain! Shipping and handling is just 50¢ per book in the U.S. and 75¢ per book in Canada.* I understand that accepting the 2 free books and gifts places me under no obligation to buy anything. I can always return a shipment and cancel at any time. Even if I never buy another book, the two free books and gifts are mine to keep forever.

225/326 HDN FEF3

Name _____ (PLEASE PRINT)

Address _____ Apt. #

City _____ State/Prov. _____ Zip/Postal Code

Signature (if under 18, a parent or guardian must sign)

### Mail to the Reader Service:
**IN U.S.A.:** P.O. Box 1867, Buffalo, NY  14240-1867
**IN CANADA:** P.O. Box 609, Fort Erie, Ontario  L2A 5X3

Not valid for current subscribers to Harlequin Desire books.

**Want to try two free books from another line?**
**Call 1-800-873-8635 or visit www.ReaderService.com.**

* Terms and prices subject to change without notice. Prices do not include applicable taxes. Sales tax applicable in N.Y. Canadian residents will be charged applicable taxes. Offer not valid in Quebec. This offer is limited to one order per household. All orders subject to credit approval. Credit or debit balances in a customer's account(s) may be offset by any other outstanding balance owed by or to the customer. Please allow 4 to 6 weeks for delivery. Offer available while quantities last.

**Your Privacy**—The Reader Service is committed to protecting your privacy. Our Privacy Policy is available online at www.ReaderService.com or upon request from the Reader Service.

We make a portion of our mailing list available to reputable third parties that offer products we believe may interest you. If you prefer that we not exchange your name with third parties, or if you wish to clarify or modify your communication preferences, please visit us at www.ReaderService.com/consumerschoice or write to us at Reader Service Preference Service, P.O. Box 9062, Buffalo, NY 14269. Include your complete name and address.

HDES11B

## Harlequin Blaze
### red-hot reads

**Sizzling fairy tales
to make every fantasy come true!**

Fan-favorite authors
## Tori Carrington and Kate Hoffmann
bring readers

*Blazing Bedtime Stories, Volume VI*

# MAID FOR HIM...

Successful businessman Kieran Morrison doesn't dare hope for
a big catch when he goes fishing. But when he wakes up one
night to find a beautiful woman seemingly unconscious on the
deck of his sailboat, he lands one bigger than he could ever
have imagined by way of mermaid Daphne Moore.
But is she real? Or just a fantasy?

# OFF THE BEATEN PATH

Greta Adler and Alex Hansen have been friends for seven years.
So when Greta agrees to accompany Alex at a mountain retreat
owned by a client, she doesn't realize that Alex has a different
path he wants their relationshiop to take.
But will Greta follow his lead?

**Available April 2012 wherever books are sold.**

www.Harlequin.com

HB79679

*Taft Bowman knew he'd ruined any chance he'd had for happiness with Laura Pendleton when he drove her away years ago...and into the arms of another man, thousands of miles away. Now she was back, a widow with two small children...and despite himself, he was starting to believe in second chances.*

*Harlequin Special® Edition® presents a new installment in USA TODAY bestselling author RaeAnne Thayne's miniseries,* THE COWBOYS OF COLD CREEK.

*Enjoy a sneak peek of* A COLD CREEK REUNION

*Available April 2012 from Harlequin® Special Edition®*

A younger woman stood there, and from this distance he had only a strange impression, as though she was somehow standing on an island of calm amid the chaos of the scene, the flashing lights of the emergency vehicles, shouts between his crew members, the excited buzz of the crowd.

And then the woman turned and he just about tripped over a snaking fire hose somebody shouldn't have left there.

Laura.

He froze, and for the first time in fifteen years as a firefighter, he forgot about the incident, his mission, just what the hell he was doing here.

Laura.

Ten years. He hadn't seen her in all that time, since the week before their wedding when she had given him back his ring and left town. Not just town. She had left the whole damn country, as if she couldn't run far enough to get away from him.

Some part of him desperately wanted to think he had made some kind of mistake. It couldn't be her. That was just some other slender woman with a long sweep of honey-blond hair and big, blue, unforgettable eyes. But no. It was definitely Laura. Sweet and lovely.

Not his.

He was going to have to go over there and talk to her. He didn't want to. He wanted to stand there and pretend he hadn't seen her. But he was the fire chief. He couldn't hide out just because he had a painful history with the daughter of the property owner.

Sometimes he hated his job.

*Will Taft and Laura be able to make the years recede...or is the gulf between them too broad to ever cross?*

*Find out in*
*A COLD CREEK REUNION*
*Available April 2012 from Harlequin® Special Edition®*
*wherever books are sold.*

Celebrate the 30th anniversary
of Harlequin® Special Edition® with a bonus story
included in each Special Edition® book in April!